THE STORY OF
MY EXPERIMENTS WITH TRUTH

THE STORY OF MY EXPERIMENTS WITH TRUTH

Mohandas Karamchand Gandhi

First published in 2020

Om KIDZ | Om Books International

Corporate & Editorial Office
A-12, Sector 64, Noida 201 301
Uttar Pradesh, India
Phone: +91 120 477 4100
Email: editorial@ombooks.com
Website: www.ombooksinternational.com

Sales Office
107, Ansari Road, Darya Ganj,
New Delhi 110 002, India
Phone: +91 11 4000 9000
Email: sales@ombooks.com
Website: www.ombooks.com

© Om Books International 2020

Retold by Swayam Ganguly

ALL RIGHTS RESERVED. No part of this book may be reproduced or transmitted in any form by any means, electronic or mechanical, including photocopying and recording, or by any information storage and retrieval system, except as may be expressly permitted in writing by the publisher.

ISBN: 978-93-5376-558-3

Printed in India

10 9 8 7 6 5 4 3 2 1

Contents

1.	Childhood	7
2.	The Husband	19
3.	High School	29
4.	Tragedy	39
5.	My Father's Death	49
6.	Religion	59
7.	The Outcaste	65
8.	London	73
9.	Back in India	83
10.	South Africa	91
11.	Settled in Natal	101
12.	Homeward Bound	111
13.	The Storm	117
14.	Brahmacharya	125
15.	The Boer War	131
16.	A Month with Gokhale	139
17.	South African Diaries	145
18.	The War	155
19.	Back to India	163
20.	Religious Excursions	171
21.	Champaran	179
22.	Penetrating the Villages	187
23.	The Kheda Satyagraha	197
24.	Rescued from Death	203
25.	The Rowlatt Bills	209
26.	Congress Initiation	217
27.	Khadi and the Spinning Wheel	223
28.	The Non-Cooperation Resolution	229
29.	Farewell	233
About the Author		236
Questions		237

Chapter One

Childhood

The Gandhis trace their origins from the Bania caste and appear to have been grocers originally. But for three generations, beginning from my grandfather, they have been prime ministers in many Kathiawad States. My grandfather Uttamchand Gandhi, alias Ota Gandhi was the Diwan of Porbandar. But state intrigues forced him to leave and seek refuge in Junagadh. He saluted the Nawab of Junagadh with his left hand, and when someone demanded an explanation for the evident discourtesy, he received the following reply: "For the right hand is already pledged to Porbandar."

CHILDHOOD

After losing his first wife, Ota Gandhi married again. His first wife bore him four sons, and he had two sons by his second wife. In my childhood, I never had the feeling that the sons of Ota Gandhi were not of the same mother. Karamchand Gandhi, alias Kaba Gandhi, was the fifth of these six brothers, and Tulsidas Gandhi was the sixth. Both were prime ministers of Porbandar, in succession. Kaba Gandhi was my father. He served as prime minister in Rajkot and Vankaner and was pensioner of the Rajkot State when he passed away.

Kaba Gandhi married four times, losing his wife each time by death. His first two marriages bore him two daughters, and his last wife Putlibai, had a daughter and three sons. I was the youngest. My father loved his clan dearly, and was brave, generous and truthful. But he was also short-tempered, and I suspect, addicted to carnal pleasures. This is because he married for the fourth time when he had crossed forty. But he had earned a name for himself

both outside and within his family because of his impartiality and loyalty to the state.

My father left us very little property. The only education he had was experience. He was ignorant about history and geography, having studied only till the fifth Gujarati standard. But his expertise in handling practical affairs helped him manage difficult situations and solving the problems of hundreds. Despite having little religious training, he honed his religious skills by visiting temples and listening to religious discourses by holy men.

My mother was deeply religious and left behind a saintly memory on me. Visiting the Vaishnava temple was a daily ritual for her. She kept the most difficult vows even if she was unwell. During the Chaturmas, a four-month period during the monsoon, she took a vow of semi-fasting and fasting. Living on one meal during this period was a habit with her. Not satisfied with just that, during one Chaturmas, she fasted every alternate day.

CHILDHOOD

Another Chaturmas, she vowed not to touch food without seeing the sun. We all know that the sun does not show its face during the height of the rainy season. So, this vow was particularly difficult. When we spotted the sun, we rushed inside to tell her. But by the time she arrived, the sun had disappeared again, and she was deprived of her meal.

"That doesn't matter," she would declare cheerfully. "God does not want me to eat today!"

My mother was blessed with a strong common sense. She was well versed with matters of state, and ladies of the court thought highly of her intelligence. I still recall the intense discussions she had with the widow of the Thakore Saheb.

I was born to these parents in Porbandar on 2 October 1869. My childhood was spent there, and I recall having difficulties with multiplication tables in school. All I recall from those early days in school in Porbandar was how I called our teacher all sorts of names, along with the other boys. That strongly indicates that my intellect must have been inactive and my memory raw.

I was seven when my father arrived in Rajkot. I joined primary school there. I was a mediocre student and went to the suburban school from here, and then to high school, having already reached my twelfth year. I never lied during this period, and was shy, avoiding everyone. My books and lessons were my only friends.

I recall an incident at the examination during the first year at the high school. Mr. Giles, the Educational Inspector, had arrived on an inspection. He gave us five words to write as a spelling exercise. I had misspelt 'kettle' which was one of the words. The teacher attempted to prompt me with the end of his boot, but he failed. I was beyond the realisation that he wanted me to copy from my neighbour's slate as I thought that the teacher was there to stop us from copying.

CHILDHOOD

The result was that every boy had spelled all the words correctly, except me. I was the only one who was stupid. The teacher tried later, but I could never pick up the art of 'copying'. But I never disrespected this teacher, despite his many other flaws. I was naturally blind to the faults of elders as I was conditioned to carry out their orders, and not to examine their actions.

I recall two other incidents vividly. I hated all books other than my school books. I had to do my daily lessons as I did not want to be punished by my teacher. But I did so mechanically, and my mind was not in it. One day, I chanced to see a book my father had bought. It was a play about Shravana's devotion to his parents, and I read it with great interest. A few showmen arrived at our house at about the same time. One of the pictures they showed me was Shravana carrying his blind parents on a pilgrimage with makeshift slings on his shoulders. The picture and the book left an everlasting impression on my mind. The

painful lament of Shravana's parents after his death still lingers in my memory. The melting tune in the performance moved me greatly, and I played it on my concertina which my father had purchased for me.

Sometime later, I obtained my father's permission to watch a play called 'Harishchandra' performed by a drama company. This play captured my imagination and I could see it repeatedly. It haunted me, and I even acted like Harishchandra.

Chapter Two

The Husband

It pains me to pen down my marriage here at the age of thirteen. I pity myself and congratulate my peers who have escaped this fate. I can see no moral argument supporting such a preposterous thing as a child marriage. Make no mistake, dear reader. I was not bethrothed, but married! There are two different rites in Kathiawad- betrothal and marriage! Betrothal is an initial promise made by the parents of the girl and the boy to get them married, and it's not inviolable. If the boy dies, the girl does not become a widow. The agreement is strictly between the parents, and the children have

no part in it. Often, they aren't even informed about it. Apparently, I was betrothed thrice without my knowledge. I assume so because I was informed that two girls betrothed to me had died in turn. I recollect faintly that I was seven when I was betrothed for the third time. I don't remember being told about it. But I remember my marriage clearly.

We were three brothers, and the eldest was already married. The elders decided that my elder brother, two to three years my senior, a cousin who was a year older, and me, should all be married at the same time. Not once did they think about our welfare or consent. They just thought about their convenience and how to save money.

A Hindu marriage is far from simple. The parents of the bridegroom and bride are often ruined by wasting everything, including their time. They spend months over the preparations, and each tries to outdo the other in terms of budget and splendour. My elders obviously thought it best that the hassle of all three marriages be finished in a single go by getting all three married together. The money would also be spent once, instead of thrice. My father and uncle were both old, and we were the last children to be married. So, a triple wedding was frozen upon. At that time, all it meant to me was good clothes, drums beating, marriage processions, good food, and a strange girl as a playmate. The carnal desire came much later.

My brother and I were taken from Porbandar to Rajkot. Although my father was a Diwan, he was still a servant. The Thakore Saheb, whom he was in favour with, did not allow him to leave until the last moment. But he ordered special stage coaches for my father when he did leave, thus reducing the journey by two days. The distance from Porbandar to Rajkot is 120 miles, a cart journey of five days. My father reached in three days, but in the third stage, the cart toppled over, and my father received many injuries. He arrived bandaged all over, and all of us, including my father, lost interest in the event. But the ceremony had to be completed as the marriage dates could not be changed. I forgot my sorrow in the childish amusement of the wedding. I never thought that one day I would criticise my father harshly for marrying me off so early.

Oh! that first night! Two innocent children unknowingly thrown into the ocean of life! I had been coached by my brother's wife about my behaviour on the first night. I'm not aware who had coached my wife. We were both nervous and shy to face each other. How and what would I say to her? The coaching couldn't help me much. But coaching is not really needed in such cases. The impressions of the former birth are potent enough. Slowly, we got to know each other and spoke freely too. Although we were the same age, I lost little time to assume the authority of a husband.

But the fact that a wife should also be faithful to her husband also played in my head.

THE HUSBAND

I became a jealous husband, and although there was no reason to suspect my wife's fidelity, everyone knows that jealousy awaits no reasons. I did not allow her to go anywhere without my permission, and this led to bitter quarrels. This was almost like being imprisoned for my wife Kasturba, who was not inclined to follow my diktat. So, she went wherever and whenever she pleased. The more restraint I exercised on her, the more liberty she took. I became angrier and we didn't speak to each other. Now, it seems to me that whatever Kasturba did was completely logical. How would I have felt if she had exercised the same restraint on me? But back then, I had to establish my authority as a husband.

Dear reader, do not think that our relationship was full of bitterness, as my actions were all out of love. My goal was to make my wife an ideal wife, make her live a life of purity, and infuse her thoughts and beliefs with mine. I'm unaware if Kasturba harboured such ambitions, as she was illiterate. She was simple, independent, determined, and with me at least, shy. My passion focused on one woman, and I wanted reciprocation. But even if it wasn't reciprocated, it could not be called hopeless as there was active love on one side at least. I loved her passionately. I used to think about her even at school when our eventual meeting at nightfall would haunt me. I kept her awake till late at night with my idle chatter.

I was eager to teach Kasturba as she was illiterate. But my lustful love left no time for it as the teaching had to be done at night, and that too against her will. I did not dare to even talk to her in the presence of elders, forget teaching her. If my love had not been consumed with total lust, I'm positive she would have been a learned lady today. I could have then removed her dislike for studies.

Other than child marriage, Hindu society has another evil custom that lessens the evils of the former. Young couples are not allowed

THE HUSBAND

by their parents to stay together at length. The child-wife spends more than half her time at her father's place. We were no exception, and during the first five years of our marriage (from age thirteen to eighteen), we must have lived together for a total period of only three years. No sooner than we had spent six months together, Kasturba would receive a call-up from her parents. Such calls, although unwelcome, saved us both. I went to England when I was eighteen, and that was a lengthy and healthy separation. But even after I returned, Kasturba and I did not live together at a stretch for more than six months. This was because I had to shuttle between Rajkot and Bombay. Then, the call from South Africa arrived, and my carnal appetite was completely freed.

Chapter Three

High School

I was attending high school when I was married. My teachers loved me, and I never received a bad certificate of progress or character. I received scholarships in the fifth and sixth standard and rupees four and ten respectively. I think good luck is responsible for this achievement more than merit in my case, because these scholarships were not open to all, but reserved for the best boys from the Sorath Division of Kathiawad. In those days, there couldn't have been many from Sorath in a class of forty to fifty.

I did not think much of my abilities. I used to be stunned when I won prizes or scholarships. I was most conscious about my character, and the smallest blemish brought tears to my eyes. A rebuke was unbearable for me. Once, I received a corporal punishment. I wept not because of the punishment, but the shame that came along with it.

I recall another incident in the seventh standard. Dorabji Edulji Gimi was the headmaster, and popular among the boys, being a good teacher, disciplinarian, and a methodical man. Under him, gymnastics and cricket were made compulsory for the boys of the upper standards. I hated both, never taking part in any exercise or sport. My shyness was the main reason for being aloof, and I now see it as wrong. I was under the impression then that gymnastics had nothing to do with education. Today, I'm aware that physical training is as important as mental training in the curriculum.

However, I was not totally averse to exercise. Having read about the advantages of long walks in the open air, I had formed the habit of taking long walks, a habit that remains. Another reason for shirking gymnastics was the desire to serve my father. The timing of compulsory exercise conflicted with this service. But Mr. Gimi would not accept my plea to be excused from gymnastics.

One Saturday, when we had school in the morning, we had to reach school for gymnastics at four in the afternoon. I did not own a watch and was deceived by the clouds that day. I reached when all the boys had left, and the next day Mr. Gimi observed my absence after inspecting the rolls. He did not believe my explanation and asked me to pay a fine. The fact that I had been accused of lying hurt me more than anything else! How would I prove my innocence? I cried in pain. I recall faintly that I managed to get the fine remitted. I was also excused from exercise

as my father wrote to the headmaster, stating that he wanted me home straight after school.

I am still suffering the price for having neglected something else other than exercise. Somehow, I got the idea that good handwriting was not an essential part of education. Later, especially in South Africa, when I observed the beautiful handwriting of lawyers and men educated there, I was ashamed that I had neglected my handwriting. I realised that bad handwriting was a sign of imperfect education. It was too late to improve mine when I tried. Let every young man and woman realise that good handwriting is a necessary part of education. I also feel that children should be taught the art of drawing before they learn how to write. The child should learn his letters by observation, on seeing flowers, birds, etc., and only once he has learnt to draw objects, should he learn handwriting. Then, he will have a beautifully formed hand.

I had lost a year at school because of my marriage. The teacher wanted to make my loss good by skipping a class, a privilege bestowed to industrious boys. Hence, I only had six months in the third standard, and was promoted to the fourth standard after the exams. From the fourth standard onwards, English became the medium of teaching for most subjects. I was totally at sea! Geometry was a new subject in which I found myself weak, and studying in English made it even more difficult. I could not follow the teacher although he taught very well.

I would lose heart often and contemplate returning to the third standard. I felt that the packing of studies for two years into a single year was too ambitious. However, this would discredit both me and my teacher as he had recommended my promotion on seeing my capability. So, this fear made me hold on to my post.

One day, when I reached the thirteenth proposition of Euclid with great difficulty, the sheer simplicity of geometry was revealed to me. A subject that required the use of one's reasoning powers couldn't be difficult after all. After that, geometry has been both simple and interesting for me.

Sanskrit, however, proved to be a much more difficult task. Unlike geometry, there was a lot to memorise in Sanskrit that also began from the fourth standard. After reaching the sixth, I began losing hope. The teacher was a hard taskmaster who forced the boys. There was a rivalry between the Sanskrit and the Persian teachers. The Persian teachers were said to be lenient and good in comparison, and tempted by the good things I heard, I sat in the Persian class one day. The Sanskrit teacher was saddened and called me to his side.

"How can you forget that you are the son of a Vaishnava father?" he exclaimed. "Don't you want to learn the language of your own religion? Why don't you come to me if you are facing any difficulty? I will teach you Sanskrit the best I can."

HIGH SCHOOL

I was ashamed as he was so kind, and I am grateful to Krishnashankar Pandya today. If he hadn't instilled the interest in Sanskrit, I wouldn't have taken any interest in our sacred books. Every Hindu boy and girl should have sound Sanskrit knowledge. All Indian curricula should have Hindi, Sanskrit, Persian, Arabic and English, apart from the vernacular of course. I'm positive that learning so many languages would not be bothersome, but a pleasure. If one possesses scientific knowledge of one language, picking up other languages becomes comparatively easy. One who wants to learn good Urdu must learn Persian and Arabic, just as one who wants to learn good Gujarati, Bengali, Marathi, or Hindi, must learn Sanskrit.

Chapter Four

Tragedy

I had only two intimate friends at the high school. One of these friendships didn't last long, although my first friend forsook me because I made friends with the other. I regard this second friendship as a tragedy of my life. This friend was initially my elder brother's companion and classmate. My family members, including my wife, warned me that I was in bad company. Although I was too proud to heed my wife's warning, I could not ignore that of my mother and eldest brother. But they let me have my own way.

This friend informed me that many of our teachers were secretly consuming meat and wine, along with many famous people from Rajkot. Some high-school boys were also part of the party. I was surprised and hurt and asked him the reason.

"We are weak because we do not eat meat," he explained. "Why do the English rule over us? Because they are meat-eaters. See how strong I am and how fast I sprint. All because I'm a meat-eater. Meat-eaters don't have boils or tumours, and they heal quickly even if they do. You think our teachers and the famous people who eat meat are fools? You should try it too! See the strength it gives."

My elder brother had already fallen prey to this friend's coaxing and was a meat-eater now. He supported this argument, and I realised that both were stronger and more well-built than me. Besides, I was a coward who was afraid of the dark, ghosts and serpents. I was ashamed that my wife was braver than me. My friend

TRAGEDY

knew these weaknesses I had, and convinced me that he could hold serpents in his hand, defy thieves, and was unafraid of ghosts because of eating meat.

A work of Gujarati poet Narmad was very popular amongst us schoolboys. It went:

> Behold the mighty Englishman
> He rules the Indian small,
> Because being a meat-eater
> He is five cubits tall.

I was finally convinced that if the entire country took to meat-eating, we could overcome the English. A day was fixed for the experiment, but in absolute secrecy, as we Gandhis were staunch Vaishnavas. Jainism was strong in Gujarat, and Jains and Vaishnavas opposed meat-eating whole-heartedly. The fear of shocking my staunch parents and my devotion to truth made me extra cautious. But I was firm in the belief that one needed to consume meat to be strong and to defeat the British.

The day finally arrived when we went to

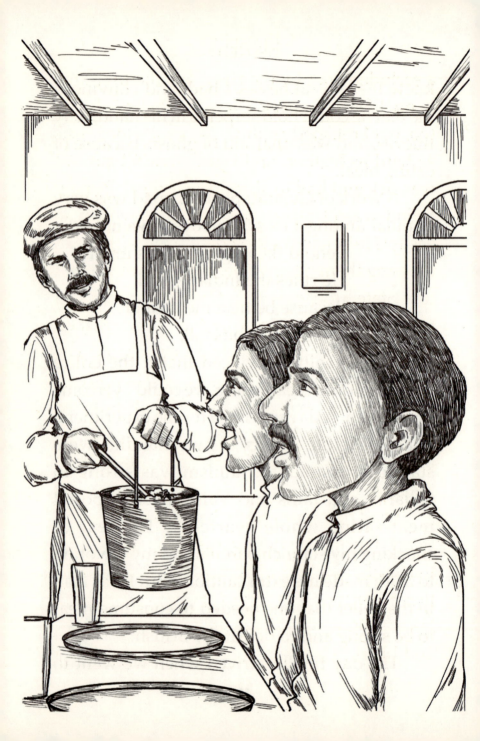

TRAGEDY

a secluded spot by the river. For the first time in my life I saw-meat! There was baker's bread too, but I relished neither. The goat's meat was as hard as leather, and I just couldn't eat it. I was sick and had to abandon the meal. But my friend wasn't a man who would give up so easily. He began cooking delicacies with meat, dressing them neatly. The venue now changed to a State House, with a fine dining hall and tables and chairs, where my friend had reached an arrangement with the chief cook. This had its effect, and I became a meat lover. This carried on for a year, but we had only half-a-dozen meat feasts. This was because of the expenses involved as well as the limited availability of the State House.

I had no money to pay for these expensive treats, but my friend always managed to find the funds, god knows from where. But even his means seemed limited as the feasts began to lessen. Dinner was impossible after these feasts, and I had to lie to my mother, stating, "There is something wrong with my digestion," or, "I have no appetite today!"

But these lies gnawed at my heart, and I finally decided to abstain from meat-eating till my parents were alive, rather than causing them pain on discovery. Since that day, I have never returned to meat. Although I abandoned meat, I could not abandon my friend. I was still unaware of the destruction that was coming because of my passion to reform him.

The same friend's company would have led to me being unfaithful to my wife. He took me to a brothel and sent me inside a room with instructions. It was prearranged, and he had already paid the bill. But I was struck deaf and dumb as I sat on the woman's bed. I could not utter a word, and she lost patience, showing me the door after abuses and insults. I felt as if my manhood had been insulted but was grateful to God later for having saved me. I can recall four other incidents in my life when I was similarly saved because of sheer luck. I say this because

TRAGEDY

the carnal desire was dominant in me and only Providence saved me.

Despite these incidents, I was still blind to the ill-effects of my friend's company. It was only later that my eyes were opened after many such bitter experiences. He also caused differences between me and my wife, fanning suspicions in my mind about her character. I am guilty of having indulged in violence and paining my wife because of his information. Maybe only a Hindu wife will endure such pain and wrong. A wrongly suspected servant will leave his job, a son would leave his father's home, and a friend would end the friendship. If the wife suspects her husband, she'll keep quiet. But if the husband suspects the wife, she is ruined. She has nowhere to turn to and cannot even seek divorce in a law-court. I can never forgive myself for causing so much pain to my wife.

Only when I understood the concept of Ahimsa, in all its layers, was the suspicion

TRAGEDY

totally rooted out. I realised the glory of Brahmacharya and concluded that a wife is more of a husband's companion and equal partner rather than a bonded slave. She's as free as her husband to choose her own destiny. When I look back now, I am repulsed at my actions towards my wife, and regret the blind faith displayed to my friend.

Chapter Five

My Father's Death

A relative and I became addicted to smoking after watching our uncle smoke. Because of a lack of money, we used the cigarette stumps thrown away by our uncle. Then, we began stealing coppers from the servant's pocket money to buy cigarettes. One day, we heard that stalks of a certain plant were porous and could be smoked like cigarettes. We began this kind of smoking.

Finally, one day, out of sheer disgust, we decided to commit suicide. We went into the jungle to look for Dhatura seeds, learning that they were effective poison. But after getting

them, our courage failed us, and we only dared to swallow a couple of seeds. Both of us composed ourselves and dismissed all thoughts of death.

I realised that it was not as easy to commit suicide as it is to think about it. But the thought of suicide resulted in our giving up smoking and stealing for it. After that, I have never desired to have a smoke. In fact, I consider the habit of smoking barbarous, dirty and harmful, and cannot understand its rage throughout the world.

But I was guilty of further theft sometime later. I think I was twelve when I stole those coppers. But this other theft was committed when I was fifteen, when I stole a bit of gold from my brother's armlet. This armlet was made of solid gold and it was easy to clip a bit out of it. I did this to clear a debt of twenty-five rupees that this brother had run into. But I was very guilty after this debt was cleared and vowed never to steal again.

MY FATHER'S DEATH

I decided to write out a confession to my father and ask for his forgiveness. I wrote this on a piece of paper and handed it to him. Not only did I confess my guilt, but also asked for adequate punishment, pledging never to steal again in the future. My father read the note, and his tears wet the paper. I cried as well, but his pearl-drops of love cleansed my heart, washing away my sins.

This was an object-lesson in Ahimsa for me. Then, I saw a father's love in the action, but today I realise it to be pure Ahimsa. When such Ahimsa becomes all-embracing, it transforms everything it touches. Its power is limitless. I never thought my father could be capable of such sublime forgiveness. I had thought he would be angry. But he was so peaceful because of my clean confession. A clean confession along with the promise of never committing the sin again, when offered before someone who had the right to receive it, is the purest form of repentance.

In my sixteenth year, my father was bed-ridden, suffering from a fistula. He was attended by me, my mother, and an old servant. My duties included dressing the wound and making and giving my father his medicines. I massaged his legs each night, retiring only when he was asleep. My time was divided between school and attending to my father. My wife was expecting a baby as well this time, and this was a double shame for me, as I didn't restrain myself. This was because I was still a student, and because carnal lust shouldn't have dominated my senses when I had a duty to serve my ailing father. I was relieved after my duties ended in my father's room and headed straight to my bedroom.

My father's condition was deteriorating every day, as Ayurvedic physicians, hakims, and local quacks failed. Even an English surgeon had tried his skills, recommending a surgical operation by a well-known Bombay surgeon. But the family physician opposed this

MY FATHER'S DEATH

move, and the family seconded him. I think my father would have been saved if the operation had been done. That dreadful night, my uncle was in Rajkot. I recall that he rushed home after receiving news that my father's condition had worsened. The brothers had a deep attachment, and my uncle would sit by my father's bed the entire day, insisting that he sleep beside him at night, sending us all away. That night, at 11 p.m., my uncle offered to relieve me, and I headed straight to my bedroom.

My wife was fast asleep, the poor thing! But how could she sleep when I was there? I woke her up, but after five or six minutes, a knock on the door startled me.
"Get up," the servant said. "Father is very ill!" I guessed what he meant and jumped out of bed. "What's the matter? Tell me!" I demanded.
"Father is no more!" he declared.

So, it was all over! I was so sad, ashamed and miserable at the same time. I should have been next to my father in his last moments, and

MY FATHER'S DEATH

not in my bedroom. I ran to my father's room. My uncle, on count of his devotion to my father, had the honour of being with my father in his last moments. The shame of being in lust when my father was dying is a blot in my memory that I've never been able to erase. It took me a long time to break free from the shackles of lust, and I had to cross many hurdles to achieve it. Before I end this chapter, let me tell you that the child that was born to my wife did not live for more than three to four days. Let all married men be warned by my example.

Chapter Six

Religion

From my sixth to my sixteenth year, I was taught many things in school, except religion. I'm using the term 'religion' in a broader perspective, meaning knowledge of self or self-realisation. I was born in the Vaishnava faith, but going to the Haveli was never appealing to me, as I disliked its pomp and glitter. Rumours of immoral practices there also led to my loss of interest.

But I got what I needed from an old servant of the family, a nurse. She suggested to me that I should repeat the Ramanama to get rid of my fear of ghosts and spirits. Thanks

RELIGION

to this good soul, reciting the Ramanama is a habit now. I think the Ramayana of Tulsidas is the greatest devotional book. I heard the Bhagawad much later and wished that I had heard it in my childhood to develop an even greater liking for it.

In Rajkot, I developed a tolerance for all branches of Hinduism and its sister religions at a very early age. Jain monks visited my father, who also had Musalman and Parsi friends. I had a toleration for all faiths at that time except Christianity because Christian missionaries would stand in a corner near the high school, showering abuse on Hindus and their gods. I also heard about a Hindu being converted to Christianity. At the time when he was baptised, he was made to eat beef and drink liquor. I also heard that the new convert had begun abusing his old religion, its customs and people. All these things made me dislike Christianity then.

I came across Manusmriti, or The Laws of Manu, in my father's collection one day. The

RELIGION

story of creation did not impress me much, but what it did was inclined me towards aethism. Manusmriti also supported Ahimsa, a belief strong in me. But I felt it was moral to kill serpents, bugs, and other insects. But one thing was deeply rooted in me- morality is the basis of all things, and truth is the substance of all morality. Truth became my only objective, and the return of good for evil became my motto.

Chapter Seven

The Outcaste

In 1887, I passed the matriculation examination. The two centres allocated were Ahmedabad and Bombay. Poor students preferred the centre that was cheaper and nearer, and I was no exception. This was my first journey from Rajkot to Ahmedabad all alone. Now, my elders wanted me to go to college. I chose the Samaldas College at Bhavnagar over the Bombay college as it was cheaper. But I was totally lost there as everything was so tough. I could not follow as I was so raw and as the professors were so good. I returned home after the first term.

    Mavji Dave was a shrewd and learned Brahmin who was also a good family friend.

He was the one who suggested that I be sent to England, as it was easy to become a barrister there.

"He will return in three years from England, whereas here it will take him four to five years to get his B.A. degree," he explained. "The expenses incurred in England won't be more than five thousand rupees, and once he's back, he can get the Diwanship for the asking. I strongly advise that Mohandas be sent to England this year only. My son Kevalram has many friends there, and he will give Mohandas notes of introduction."

My elder brother was perplexed, as he was unsure if a young man like me should travel abroad alone. How would he manage the funds? My mother was also averse to the idea of parting with me. My brother had an idea.

"We have some stake in the Porbandar state," he declared to me. "The administrator, Mr. Lely has high regard for our family. He might recommend some State help to further your education in England."

THE OUTCASTE

My journey to Porbandar was a five-day bullock-cart journey as there were no railways those days. I hired a bullock-cart to Dhoraji and took a camel from there to reach Porbandar a day earlier. I wrote to Mr. Lely, who asked me to come and see him.

"Pass your B.A., and then come and see me," he declared, refusing to offer any help. I returned to Porbandar and told my family all that had taken place. Joshiji advised taking a loan if needed. I spoke about selling my wife's ornaments as that would fetch two to three thousand rupees. My brother said he would arrange the money somehow.

My mother was against the idea, hearing somewhere that young men got lost in England, and that they couldn't live there without meat and alcohol.

"I swear not to touch those things," I reassured her, adding that Joshiji wouldn't have let me go if there was so much danger in England. My mother decided to consult Bechara

Swamiji, a Jain monk and another family adviser. He made me take three vows before allowing me to go. I vowed not to touch wine, women and meat. Finally, my mother gave her consent.

The high school gave me a grand send-off as it was uncommon for a boy from Rajkot to travel to England. I started on my first journey from Rajkot to Bombay, accompanied by my brother. Leaving behind my family, my wife, and a baby of a few months, I set off for Bombay. After arrival, we learnt that the Indian Ocean was rough in June and that I should not set sail till November. A gale had just sunk a steamer. My brother left me behind in Bombay and left for Rajkot, leaving an allowance for me.

Meanwhile, my caste-people were angry that I was going to England, and I was summoned to attend a general meeting of the caste to be brought to book! No Modh Bania had dared to travel to England till now, after all. I went fearlessly to meet the Seth- the community headman. To his accusation, I replied that I didn't think that it was against our religion to travel to England as I wanted to go there for further studies rather than anything else.

"You will disregard the orders of the caste?" he demanded.

"I don't think the caste should interfere in my personal matter," I replied. The furious Seth swore at me and declared, "This boy is an outcaste from today. Anyone helping him or seeing him off to the dock shall be punished with a fine of one rupee four annas."

This incident only made me more determined to go to England. I heard that a Junagadh vakil was leaving for England on 4th September. I decided to avail this opportunity, and wrote to my brother, who agreed. But my brother-in-law in Bombay refused to give me the money, saying he did not wish to lose caste because of the Seth's order. Finally, a friend gave me the loan I

THE OUTCASTE

wanted, agreeing to recover the money from my brother later. I bought the passage with a part of the money and purchased appropriate clothes. My berth was procured in the same cabin as the Junagadh vakil, Sjt. Mazumdar. He was a mature, experienced man while I was an eighteen-year-old without any experience of the world. I sailed from Bombay on 4th September.

Chapter Eight

London

Although I was not sea-sick, I became shy and fidgety each day. I was not used to speaking in English, and all the other passengers except Sjt. Mazumdar were English. I could not understand them when they spoke to me, and when I could, I could not speak to them properly. I didn't know the use of knives and forks and was not bold enough to ask if the dishes were free of meat. So, I always had my meals in the cabin, going to the deck only when there were few people.

An English passenger, much older, took kindly to me. He drew me into conversation first, advising me later to come to the table to eat. He laughed at my resistance to meat, saying that it was so cold in England that one had to eat meat. We reached Southampton, I think on a Saturday. The four notes of introduction I had were to Dr. P.J. Mehta, Sjt. Dalpatram Shukla, Prince Ranjitsinhji, and Dadabhai Nairoji. Sjt. Mazumdar and I went to the Victoria Hotel as advised by someone on board. I had wired Dr. Mehta from Southampton, and he called in the evening. He recommended that I live with a private family as a hotel was expensive.

A Sindhi fellow-passenger offered to find rooms for us, and we left the hotel on Monday as soon as we received our baggage. Even in the new rooms, I was uncomfortable and totally homesick. I would cry at night thinking of my mother, and I couldn't share my sorrow with anyone. This land was strange, and so were the people. The vegetarian vow was tough too. I could not stand England but returning to India now was impossible. I had to finish the three years, the inner voice said.

LONDON

Dr. Mehta did not approve of me staying in such rooms and insisted that I live with a family. "But before that you must serve an apprenticeship with someone," he stated, and took me there. The friend I lived with now was a good person, but he insisted that I eat meat, and I refused each time. This strengthened my belief in vegetarianism, and my mission was spreading it throughout India later.

I started reading newspapers in England, which I never did in India. To appease my friend for not eating meat, I tried becoming the English gentleman by purchasing new clothes from the Army and Navy stores. I also had to take lessons in French, dancing and elocution. But this infatuation lasted for only three months before I gave all these up. What use did I have to become an English gentleman if I did not want to stay in England?

I also decided to cut my expenses by half. I took up cheap accommodation of one room on my own rather than living with a family. I also

took up work which was walking distance away, so I could save money and gain experience at the same time. The long walks of eight to ten miles a day kept me healthy. I bought a stove and started cooking my own food, giving up tea and coffee. Lely's words that I should become a graduate first before going to him still echoed in my ears. I was learning French already, and decided to pursue Latin as well.

It was the end of my second year in England when I met two brothers, who were Theosophists. Both were unmarried and spoke to me about the Gita. They were reading Sir Edwin Arnold's translation, and invited me to read the original with them. I was ashamed as I had not read the divine poem, confessed the same, and began reading the Gita with them. The book left a deep impression on my mind and I think it's a priceless book. Apart from studying different religions, I also attempted to study atheism.

Once, in Portsmouth, for the first and last time, a woman other than my wife moved me to lust. I ran away from the scene, trembling, and spent a sleepless night in my room. I know that God saved me from sin. Not only did I leave that house, but I also left Portsmouth.

A great exhibition was supposed to be held in Paris in 1890, and I badly wanted to see Paris. So, I thought of killing two birds with one stone and went to Paris. The Eiffel Tower was of particular interest, made totally of iron, and almost 1,000 feet high. I made an economic trip, doing the sight-seeing there mostly on foot, with the help of a map. Apart from the Eiffel Tower, the ancient churches of Paris are still fresh in my memory because of their peacefulness and splendour. The wonderful Notre-Dame and the divine cathedrals could have only been constructed by people with the love of God nestled in their hearts.

The sole purpose of my England visit was being called to the bar. But two conditions had to be fulfilled first; 'keeping terms', where each term is equivalent to almost three years, and passing examinations. 'Keeping terms' denoted eating one's terms, i.e., attending at least six out of twenty-four dinners in a term. More than eating, it meant reporting at fixed hours, and being present throughout the dinner. The prices for such dinners were moderate, but it pained me that the drinks cost more than the food. I was shocked as this was sin in our country. How could people waste so much money on drink? But later, I understood why. But I failed to comprehend how these dinners prepared students better for the bar.

It took me nine months of hard labour to read through the Common Law of England. I passed my examinations and was called to the bar on 10 June 1891. I enrolled in the High Court on the 11th and sailed for home the next day. But I was still not confident to practise law. This was because I had only read about law, and not how to practice it. Besides, I knew nothing about Indian, Hindu and Mohammedan Law.

LONDON

One of my friends suggested seeking Dadabhai Naoroji's help. I had a note of introduction to him. Earlier, I was hesitant of bothering such a great man, although I used to attend his meetings. I did gather the courage to go to him and present the note of introduction. He was gracious enough to tell me to come to him whenever I needed advice. But somehow, I couldn't bring myself to do it. So, it was with great apprehension that I landed at Bombay.

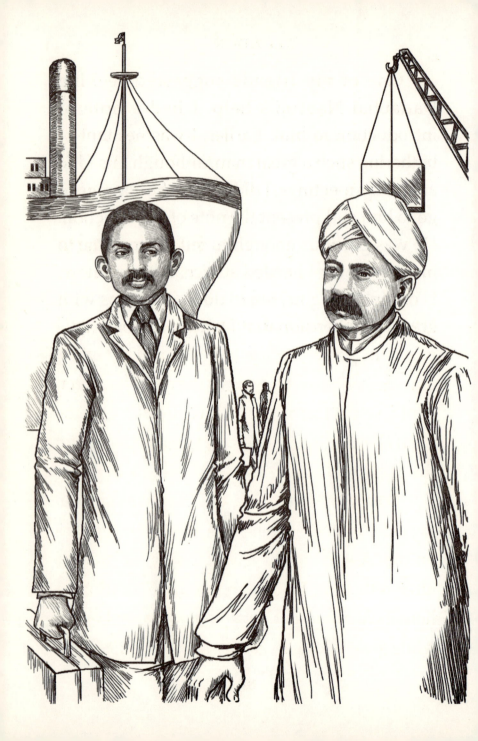

Chapter Nine

Back in India

My elder brother had come to receive me, and I was dying to see my mother. But I did not know that she had passed away, as the news had been kept a secret from me to spare the blow on me in an alien land. It was a great shock to me, and the grief was greater than my father's death.

The desire for wealth and fame was great in my elder brother, and he had pinned great hopes on me. Assuming I'd have a swinging practice after returning from London, he had allowed household expenses to go up considerably. He also made great efforts to get my practice underway.

BACK IN INDIA

The storm in my caste over my foreign trip was still alive. The caste was divided into two camps now, one that would have me back and one that wanted me out. To please the former, my brother took me to Nasik and gave me a bath in the sacred river before going to Rajkot. Then, he gave a caste dinner there. I didn't like doing all this, but did it mechanically, reciprocating my brother's endless love for me.

I never tried to influence the section of the caste that had rejected me to take me back. Neither did I harbour any hatred for the headmen of that section. Because of my behaviour, no one from the caste has ever troubled me. Many have helped me in my work, without having any expectations from me. This goodwill is because of my non-resistance. Had I agitated and provoked them, it would have made matters worse.

My relations with my wife were still not according to my liking. I was still jealous despite

BACK IN INDIA

staying in England for so long. She still suffered because of my behaviour. Our expenses were going up, and to practice law in Rajkot would be suicidal, as no one would be able to afford my fees. Friends advised me to go to Bombay to gain experience in the High Court and study Indian law. So, I went. The study of Indian Law was a tedious task, and with expenses mounting in Bombay every month, I took up Mamibai's case. It was a small case, but with a condition. I had to pay a commission to the tout, which even big lawyers did. I simply refused to do so but got the case all the same. It was an easy case, expected to get over in a day and so, I charged Rs. 30.

My debut in the Small Causes Court was a disaster. I was tongue-tied and could not think of a question to ask. I must have been a laughing stock before the judge and the other vakils. I told the agent I could not conduct the case. He'd better engage Patel and take the fee back from

me. Mr. Patel was then engaged for a fee of Rs. 51, and the case was child's play to him.

I decided I would take up a teacher's job, and as my English was good enough, I decided to apply for the post of an English teacher in a famous high school. I was dejected after they refused me because I was not a graduate. I decided to return to Rajkot and set up my small office there. I did much better in Rajkot, earning three hundred rupees every month drafting memorials and applications. My first encounter with a British officer ended up in him insulting me and throwing me out of his office. The incident was a big shock to me. But that shock changed the course of my life!

Chapter Ten

South Africa

The political struggles between states, corruption, and intrigue were becoming depressing for me. The atmosphere was so poisonous that it was difficult for someone like me to remain unscathed. The quarrel with the sahib also stood between me and my practice now.

Then, a Meman firm from Porbandar wrote to my brother with a job offer for me: "We have a big firm in South Africa, and we have a big case in court, our claim being 40,000 pounds. This case has been going on for a long time, and we have engaged the services of the best vakils and barristers. If you send your brother there, it will be a mutually beneficial association. He will also have the advantage of seeing a new world and making new acquaintances."

I was tempted, as my services would be required only for a year. Besides, I would not have any expenses there and would be paid a sum of 105 pounds for my services. Although this meant going to South Africa not as a barrister but as a servant of the firm, I agreed because I was desperate to leave India. The money earned would help my family. I just felt sad to part with my wife as we had had another baby. Our love was becoming purer from lust, and I was her teacher now, albeit indifferent. But the attraction of South Africa made this separation secondary. I was in for disappointment when I reached Bombay as there were no berths left on the boat sailing for Natal. The agent offered me a place as deck passenger which I refused. How could a barrister travel as a deck passenger? I decided to board the boat and meet the captain. I learnt that the Governor-General of Mozambique was travelling by this boat, and all the berths had been taken.

After a lot of requests, the Captain offered me an extra berth in his cabin, normally not reserved for passengers. We reached the first port of call, Lamu in thirteen days, where we halted for three to four hours. The next port was Mombasa, and then Zanzibar. We halted here for about ten days, and the next call was Mozambique. We reached Natal at the end of May.

Durban is the port of Natal and is also known as Port Natal. As we landed, I saw that Indians were not much respected here. Those who knew the agent, Abdulla Sheth, behaved snobbishly with him. I was put up in a room next to Abdulla Sheth's. The Indians here were divided into various groups. The first was the one of Musalman merchants, who termed

themselves 'Arabs'. The second was of the Hindu clerks, and the third of the Parsi clerks who would call themselves 'Persians'. But the largest class was made up of Tamil, Telugu and North Indian labourers. These had indentured labourers and freed labourers. The former was in agreement to serve for five years, and the other three classes only had business relations with them. The English called them 'coolies', and hence, I was known as 'coolie barrister'. The original name of 'coolie' was forgotten as all Indians began to be addressed as 'coolies'.

Among the indentured Indians, there were Hindus, Musalmans and Christians. The last class was the children of indentured Indians who had converted to Christianity. The majority of these worked as waiters in hotels. After seven to eight days of my arrival, I was summoned to Pretoria with a first-class seat booked for me. After the train reached Maritzburg, the capital

of Natal, a passenger entered, and looked me up and down. He appeared disturbed that a 'coloured man' was in the compartment. He left, returning with two officials. A third official arrived, ordering me to go to the van compartment. "I have a first-class ticket," I protested. But they insisted that I leave and threatened to call a police constable. I refused, and a police constable arrived. He took me by the hand and pushed me out. My luggage followed suit and the train steamed away. I took refuge in the lightless waiting-room as it was very cold in winter. *Should I fight for my rights or return to India?* I thought. *Should I travel to Pretoria ignoring the insults? I would be branded a coward if I returned to India without fulfilling my duty. I would try and root out the disease of colour prejudice instead!*

So, I decided to take the next train to Pretoria. The train reached Charlestown in the morning.

In those days, there was no railway between Charlestown and Johannesburg. There was only a stage-coach and I purchased a ticket for it. The 'leader', as the white man in charge of the coach was called, ordered me not to be seated with the white passengers. He gave me a seat on the side of the coachbox instead. I decided to swallow the insult rather than be thrown off the coach. At three o clock, the leader asked me to vacate the seat. He probably wanted to have a smoke and some fresh air. Taking a dirty sack-cloth, he placed it on the footboard and asked me to sit on it. I protested, and he started boxing my ears heavily. As he tried to drag me down, I held on to the brass rails for support. He was strong, and I was weak. Finally, I was released as a few passengers pitied my situation and asked the man to leave me alone. The man threatened to get even with me once we reached Standerton.

I was relieved to reach Standerton after

SOUTH AFRICA

dark as I saw Indian faces. These friends had come to receive me on Abdulla's instructions. I was taken to Isa Seth's shop where the Seth and his clerks heard my story sympathetically. I travelled to Johannesburg by coach and reached Pretoria by train from there. As I had arrived on a Sunday, there was no one to receive me. I wondered where to go as no hotel would accept me. The ticket collector was polite but not helpful. An American Negro offered to help and took me to a hotel which accommodated me. I had a hearty dinner there. The next morning, I met the attorney, Mr. Baker, whom I was supposed to work with. He found me cheap lodgings at 35 shilling a week. The landlady here was a poor woman who was a good person.

The year's stay in Pretoria was valuable for me. I learnt public work, developed my legal skills, and enriched the religious spirit within me.

Chapter Eleven

Settled in Natal

After the case concluded, I left Pretoria to return to Durban and prepared to go back home. Abdulla Sheth gave a farewell party in my honour at Sydenham. After arriving there, I read something astonishing in a newspaper. It was about the Franchise Bill then before the House of Legislature, which aimed at depriving the Indians to elect members of the Natal Legislative Assembly.

"If this bill becomes a law, it will make things very difficult for us," I informed Abdulla Sheth. "It will be the first nail in the coffin as it strikes at the root of our self-respect."

He asked for my advice as the other guests heard our conversation. "May I suggest what can be done?" one of the guests chimed in. "Cancel your passage to India, stay on for a month, and we will fight under your leadership."

All the guests asked Abdulla Sheth that I be detained. The Sheth was a shrewd man. "You have every right to detain him as I do," he said. "But he is a barrister. How will we pay his fees?" This hurt me, and I told him that I couldn't take fees for public work. "I'm ready to stay on for another month," I said. "But funds will be needed for sending telegrams, printing literature, consulting local attorneys and law books."
A chorus of voices was heard now that money would be arranged, and I would have as many men I would need. The dinner was transformed into a working committee. Thus, the foundations of my life in South Africa was raised, and the seeds for the fight for national self-respect were sown.

In 1893, Sheth Haji Muhammad Haji Dada was considered the foremost leader of the

SETTLED IN NATAL

Indian community in Natal. Even though Sheth Abdulla Haji was the financial chief, Sheth Haji Muhammad was always given first place in public affairs. So, a meeting was held under his presidentship to oppose the Franchise Bill. Volunteers were enrolled, including Christian Indian youths, local merchants and clerks from big firms who were themselves surprised to be doing public work. Class, religious and race distinctions were forgotten in the face of the calamity faced by the Indian community, as all were alike as servants of the motherland now.

The bill was in its second reading and the first thing we did was send a telegram to the Speaker of the Assembly, requesting him to postpone further discussion on the bill. A similar telegram was sent to the Premier, Sir John Robinson. We were very happy when we received a prompt reply from the Speaker that discussion on the bill would be postponed for two days. The petition to be presented to the Legislative Assembly was drawn up and it was

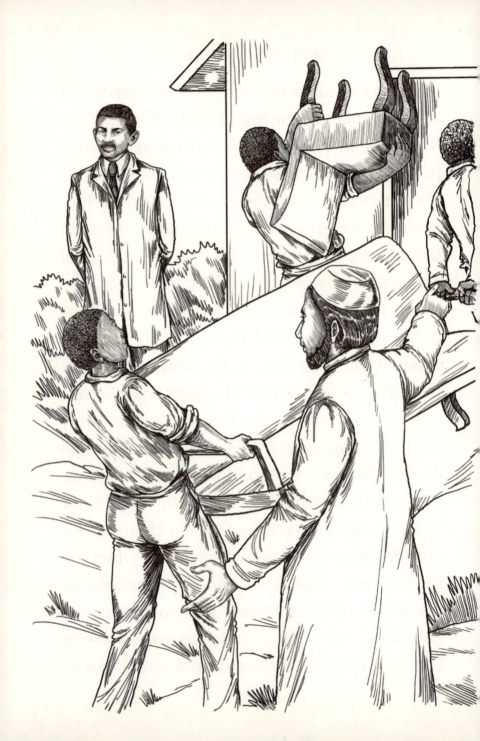

SETTLED IN NATAL

proposed to obtain maximum signatures in a single night. Volunteers worked throughout the night as merchants hired carriages. The newspapers wrote about us favourably and it was discussed in the House. But the Bill was still passed. We were disappointed, but the community was united now, and we submitted a monster petition to Lord Ripon, the Secretary of State for the Colonies. In a fortnight, ten thousand signatures were obtained, and this time, even villages were covered. The Times of India and The London Times supported our claims, and we began to harbour hopes of the bill getting vetoed. I couldn't leave Natal now as people were dependant on my presence and services here. I started looking for a house to stay, and suddenly realised that I couldn't afford one. But I refused to accept a salary for public work. Then, a solution was reached as twenty merchants gave me retainers for a year of their legal work. Dada Abdullah also gifted me some furniture from the money for my farewell gift. The Congress was the very life of India and disliked by the Conservatives in England. I recommended that our new organisation be called the Natal Indian Congress.

One day, a Tamil man called Balasundaram came to me in tattered clothes. He was crying, and his mouth was bleeding with two front teeth broken. Balasundaram was serving his indenture with a white master who had beaten him up badly. I sent him to a doctor, taking the certificate of the nature of injury from the doctor later. Then, I took the injured Balasundaram to the Magistrate, submitting an affidavit. The angry Magistrate issued a summons against the employer. An indenture was almost like slavery, and I wanted to release Balasundaram from this evil master. One way was to cancel his indenture, which was a lengthy process, and the other to get him a new master. Otherwise, the law stated that Balasundaram would be jailed if he left his master. I managed to convince his evil master to release him and found Balasundaram a new master. Every

SETTLED IN NATAL

indentured labourer heard about this case, and I was hailed as their friend and protector.

In 1894, the Natal Government wanted to impose an annual tax of 25 pounds on the indentured Indians. I was stunned, and we decided to oppose the proposal. But I must explain the details of the tax. In 1860, the Europeans in Natal needed labour for the immense scope of work for sugarcane cultivation. As the Natal Zulus could not do this type of work, outside labour was imperative. The Natal Government contacted the Indian Government and received permission to procure Indian labour. These labourers were to sign a five-year indenture post by which they would be allowed to settle in Natal and have ownership of the land. The Indians gave more than expected as they grew many vegetables, also at a cheaper rate. They introduced the mango and entered trade too. They raised themselves from labourers to land-owners. Indian merchants followed them to Natal', settled there and engaged in trade. This alarmed the white traders, and

SETTLED IN NATAL

The initial suggestion that they be forcibly repatriated would probably not be accepted by the Government of India. So, another proposal was made where the Indian labourer would return to India after the expiry of the indenture term or he should sign a fresh indenture every two years. In case he refused to do either, he would pay an annual tax of 25 pounds. The Viceroy of India then, Lord Elgin did not agree to the 25-pound tax but did so for a poll tax of 3 pounds. I think this was a serious blunder by Lord Elgin as he had disregarded the interest of the Indians to accommodate the Natal Europeans. To levy such a tax on an average Indian family of four, where the average income was not greater than 14 s. a month was ridiculous. It took twenty long years to get this tax remitted, thanks largely to the efforts of all Indians in South Africa. It was the result of patient, relentless struggle and because the community never gave up the fight.

Chapter Twelve

Homeward Bound

In 1896, I requested permission to go home for six months to fetch my wife and children. The 3 pounds tax was a sore that had to be abolished. I landed at Calcutta after a twenty-four-day voyage. I took a train for Bombay the same day. From there, I headed to Rajkot where I worked for a month to write a pamphlet on the situation in South Africa. Ten thousand copies were printed and despatched to all leading newspapers and political leaders in India. The Pioneer took notice of it first editorially, and a summary of the article was cabled to London by Reuter. A summary of that summary,

about three lines in print, was cabled to Natal from London.

An outbreak of plague in Bombay caused panic in Rajkot. I offered my services to the State in the sanitation department which were accepted. I was absorbed into the committee and laid special stress on the cleanliness of latrines. We inspected latrines in every street, and the poor had no objection. But the upper class objected to having their latrines inspected, and we observed that their latrines were more unclean. The committee had to inspect the quarters of the untouchables also and this was a new experience for me. They had no latrines and did the job in the open. I inspected their houses instead and was delighted as everything was clean. There was no fear of an outbreak here.

I travelled to Poona from Bombay where I met Lokmanya Tilak who offered me good advice and his services whenever I needed them. Next, I met Gokhale, who welcomed me affectionately. Even though we met for the first

time, it was as if we were long lost friends. I proceeded to Madras from Poona, and then to Calcutta. I knew no one in Calcutta, but meeting Surendranath Banerji, the 'Idol of Bengal' was a must. He advised me to meet the Maharajas for help for my work in South Africa.

But none of the Maharajas were helpful. Help came from Mr. Saunders, editor of The Englishman, and we became friends as he wrote about my experiences in South Africa. I was hopeful about holding a public meeting in Calcutta when I received a cable from Durban urging me to return soon as Parliament was opening in January. I set off for Bombay. From there, I set sail for South Africa again. This time, I was accompanied by my wife, my two sons, and the son of my widowed sister.

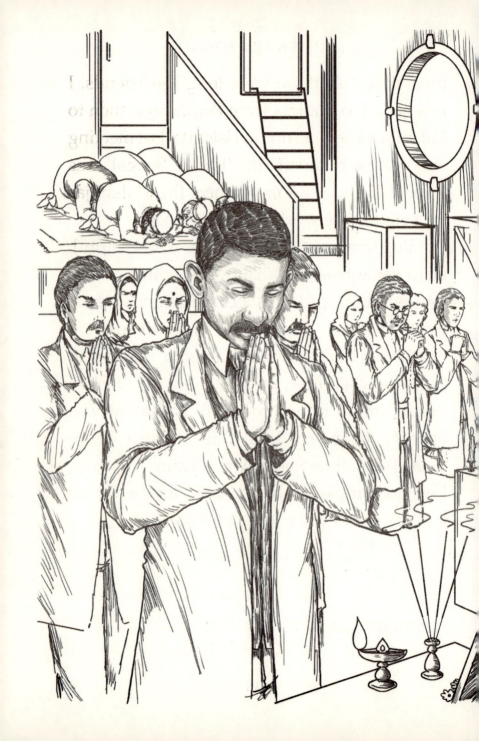

Chapter Thirteen

The Storm

The steamer was sailing directly to Natal, a journey of eighteen days. But when we were four days away from Natal, we were caught in a terrible gale. All the passengers became one as we prayed together in this terrible danger. All race and religious differences were forgotten. Thankfully, the storm passed. Little did we realise that a larger storm awaited us yet.

Because of the plague in Bombay, our ship was put on quarantine and not allowed to land at port. This was done after a doctor came and examined us. But we were quarantined not because of health issues. The white residents of Durban were agitating for our repatriation and even issuing threats. After twenty-three days, the ship finally entered the harbour. I was advised to let my wife and children drive to Mr. Rustomji's house while I walked on foot with Mr. Laughton. We started walking the journey of two miles after my family left in the car. But some youngsters recognised me and surrounded us, shouting, "Gandhi! Gandhi!" The crowd swelled up slowly and separated me from Mr. Laughton. Then, they pelted me with stones, rotten eggs and brickbats. They started kicking and beating me. The wife of the Superintendent, who knew me, was passing by. The brave lady stepped in between me and the mob with her open parasol. This checked the mob as it was impossible to hit me without harming the lady. An Indian youth had fetched the police in the meanwhile, and I was taken to the police station. But I refused to take refuge there as requested. I reached Mr. Rustomji's place without further incident. The ship's

THE STORM

doctor was there to attend to me. The whites had surrounded the house, shouting, "We must have Gandhi!"

It was suggested by the police superintendent that I escape in disguise. I did not want to do that, but finally agreed for the sake of my family, whose lives I did not want to endanger. Disguised as an Indian constable, I escaped the house in the company of two detectives, disguised as Indian merchants. The Superintendent broke the news to the crowd that I had escaped. He offered that a few representatives check the house, which they did, to discover that it was the truth. The late Mr. Chamberlain, then Secretary of State for the Colonies, cabled the Natal Government to persecute my assailants. But when Mr. Escombe called me to identify my assailants so they could be arrested, I refused. I said they could not be blamed for their actions.

"They have been wrongly led to believe that I made wrong statements about the whites in

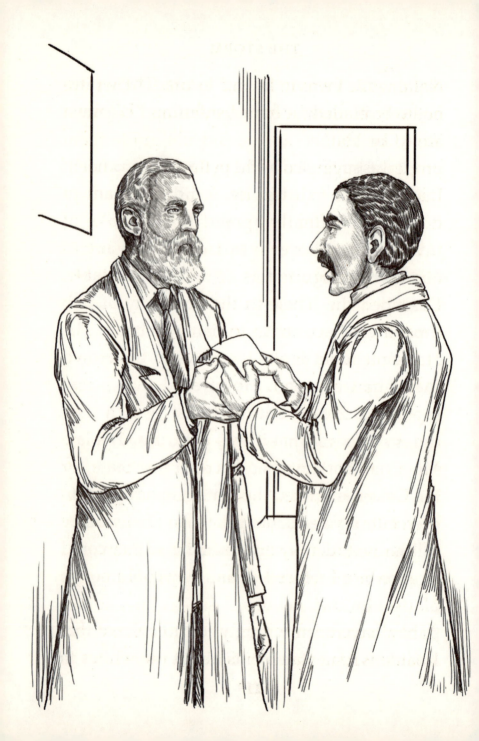

Natal while I was in India," I stated. "They are not to be blamed. It is the leaders and you who are to be blamed as you did not guide them properly, having believed in the news yourself. I do not want to book anyone as I'm sure they will be sorry after they realise their mistake."

"Can you give me your statement in writing?" Mr. Escombe requested. "I have to cable Mr. Chamberlain. There is no hurry. You may consult Mr. Laughton and your other friends."

"I do not need to consult anyone," I replied. "My decision is made."

I gave him the written statement.

I was still under the protection of the police station after two days when I was summoned by Mr. Escombe again. The day of the landing, I had been interviewed on board by a representative of The Natal Adviser, when I had managed to answer all questions and clear all charges made against me. This interview, when published and my refusal to persecute my assailants made a powerful impression on the

Durban Europeans who were ashamed of their behaviour. This enhanced the reputation of the Indian community in South Africa and only made my work easier. It also enhanced my popularity and professional practice.

But as an Indian had put up a manly fight, two bills were also introduced in the Natal Legislative Assembly. The first adversely affected Indian trade and the second imposed a strong restriction on Indian immigrants. We appealed to the Colonial Secretary who refused to interfere, and the bills became law.

Chapter Fourteen

Brahmacharya

I seriously started thinking of taking the brahmacharya vow in South Africa. I felt that the devotion of a servant to his master was a thousand times more than that of his wife towards him. It was not surprising that a wife should be devoted to her husband because of the bond between them. But to create equal devotion between master and servant required special effort. I asked myself what the ideal relation should be between me and my wife. Was it fair to make my wife the instrument of my lust just because I was faithful towards her? My lust was my weakness and the only barrier

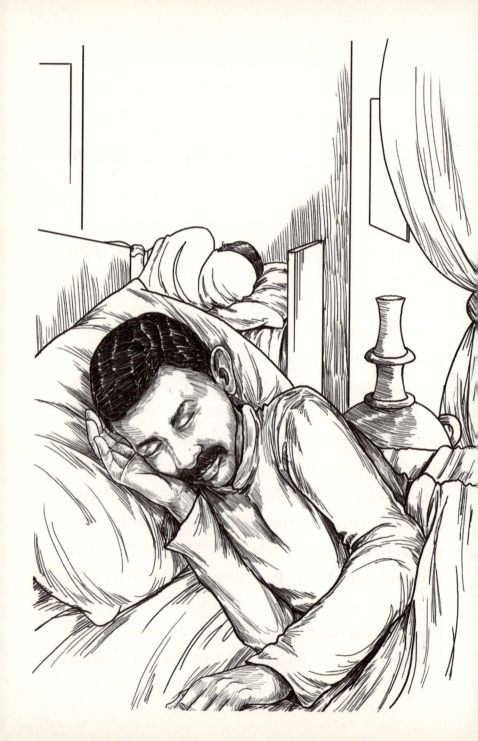

BRAHMACHARYA

between me and my brahmacharya. Yet, I failed twice because my initial motive of having no more children was weak.

I began to exercise self-control. My wife and I started sleeping in separate beds. I also realised that in public service there was no time to have or raise children. I took the vow in 1906 after consulting my wife. She had no objection, but I experienced great difficulty before taking the vow. Twenty years after taking the vow, I look back with great amazement and delight. My life has been full of happiness after taking the vow. Unknowing to me, the vow of brahmacharya had laid the very foundation of the satyagraha movement.

I understood slowly that brahmacharya led to the realisation of Brahman and that it protected the mind, body and soul. But even as I'm past fifty-six, I realise how difficult it is. It's like walking on a razor's edge where extreme vigilance is needed eternally. Control of the palate makes the observance of the vow simpler.

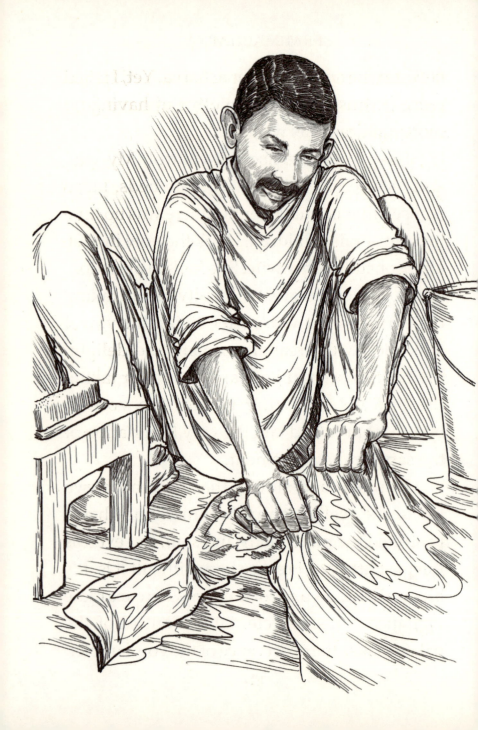

BRAHMACHARYA

A brahmachari's food should be simple, spiceless, limited, and if possible, uncooked. Fresh fruit and nuts are the best example.

I had lived a comfortable, easy life so far. Now, in my quest for a simple life, I began to cut down on expenses. I started washing clothes myself as the laundry bill was heavy. I realised the beauty of self-help, and after one incident, I decided to do away with the barber as well. An English hair-cutter in Pretoria refused to cut my hair. I was so hurt that I bought a pair of clippers and cut my hair in front of the mirror. I managed to cut the front hair but spoiled the back, evoking great laughter from my friends in court.

"Rats been at your hair, Gandhi?"

"No, the white barber refused to cut my black hair," I replied. "So, I cut it myself."

Chapter Fifteen

The Boer War

When the Boer War was declared, I sympathised completely with the Boers. But I felt that I had no right to enforce my personal convictions, and my loyalty to British rule forced me to side with the British in that war. I collected as many comrades as I could, and their services were accepted as ambulance corps. We had to march twenty to twenty-five miles per day, carrying the wounded on stretchers. We also had the honour of carrying distinguished soldiers like General Woodgate.

The corps were disbanded after six weeks' service, and our humble work was much applauded, enhancing the reputation of the Indian community. The relations with the whites were sweetest during the war, and they were friendly and thankful. I recall an instance when human nature rises above all during a moment of trial. We were marching towards camp with the wounded Lieutenant Roberts, the son of Lord Roberts, on a sultry day. Everyone was thirsting for water when we encountered a tiny brook suddenly. But who would drink first? We offered to drink after the tommies had drank their fill. But they urged us to drink first, and for a while, a pleasant competition ensued with each side inviting the other to drink first.

We also engaged in sanitary reform and famine relief in Natal after the charge that the Indian did not keep his house and surroundings clean. My bitter experiences taught me an important lesson that without endless patience, it was impossible to get work done out of people. Only the reformer wants reform, and not the society, from which nothing other than opposition is expected. Another thing that needed to be done was to awaken in the Indian settler a sense of duty to the motherland. India was a poor country, and the Indian settler had come here seeking wealth. Hence, it was his duty to give some money back to his motherland. This they did during the terrible famines of 1897 and 1899. Ever since, Indians in South Africa have always contributed generously during a national calamity.

After my war-duty, I felt I was needed more in India than in South Africa. With great difficulty, I persuaded my co-workers to release me with the condition that I would return to South Africa when I was needed. Farewell meetings were arranged by the Natal Indians everywhere, and I was showered with expensive gifts like gold, silver and diamonds. There was a gold necklace worth fifty guineas for my wife. But I could not accept these gifts and decided to return them back to the community. I had a discussion with my family,

THE BOER WAR

and my children supported my decision, stating that they did not need expensive gifts. I was delighted, but my wife opposed me, stating that the gifts would be useful for the future. She would keep them for her daughters-in-law. But after many arguments, I won over her and the gifts were deposited in a bank with a trust-deed drawn. They were to be used for the service of the community as per my wishes as well as the trustees. My wife has seen the wisdom of this move now, and I firmly believe that a public worker shouldn't accept expensive gifts.

I sailed to land in Calcutta. I decided to offer my services to the Congress office to gain some experience. Babu Bhupendranath Basu and Sjt. Ghosal were the secretaries. The former sent me to the latter, who gave me some clerical work, which I readily accepted. He gave me the job of going through his correspondence in the form of a heap of letters. I finished the job in quick time, delighting Sjt. Ghosal, who did not know me when he offered me the job. Later,

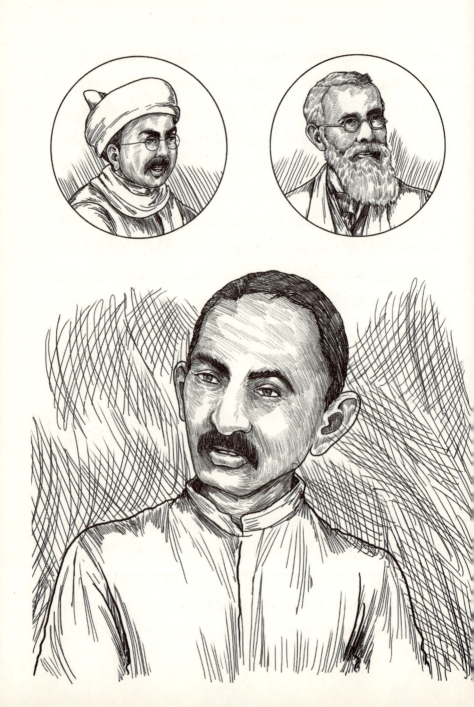

when he had made enquiries about me, he was apologetic about giving me that kind of work to do. We became good friends, and he insisted that we have lunch together.

I learnt the workings of the Congress in a few days and observed the movements of stalwarts like Gokhale and Surendranath. I also observed some loopholes like excessive use of the English language, and many doing the work of one person.

Chapter Sixteen

A Month with Gokhale

I was finally in the Congress. I read out my resolution on South Africa when Gokhale brought the matter up, and it was unanimously passed. The Congress was over, but I decided to stay on in Calcutta for a month to meet various people for my work in South Africa. I stayed with Gokhale who treated me like a younger brother. To see Gokhale at work was both a joy and an education as he devoted himself entirely to public work.

    I visited the famous Kali temple but was saddened by the slaughter of lambs there in the name of sacrifice. How could Bengal being so knowledgeable and intelligent, tolerate this slaughter? I attempted to understand Bengali culture and met many eminent Bengalis. I heard some fine Bengali music at the celebration of the Brahmo Samaj at Maharshi Devendranath Tagore's place. Since then, I have been a lover of Bengali music. After having learnt much about the Brahmo Samaj, it was impossible not to meet Swami Vivekanand. I travelled to Belur Math mostly on foot but was disappointed when I learnt that Swamiji was ill and at his Calcutta residence. So, I couldn't meet him. I met Sister Nivedita at her residence though, and was awestruck at the splendour that surrounded her. I admired her overflowing love for Hinduism.

Staying with Gokhale made my work in Kolkata very easy, and not only did I meet eminent Bengali families, but it began my intimate contact with Bengal. When it was time to separate from Gokhale, it was difficult for both of us. But my work in Calcutta was over, and I had to leave. I travelled by train

A MONTH WITH GOKHALE

to Rajkot, halting at Benares, Agra, Jaipur and Palanpur for a day each. I travelled by third-class, realising that third-class passengers travel like sheep. In Europe there is not much difference between the first-class and third-class compartments in terms of cleanliness, but here the third-class compartments were dirty. Even the third-class compartments in South Africa, reserved for Negroes, were much better than the ones here. The South African ones had sleeping accommodation and cushioned seats. In India, there was rubbish all over the compartments, with constant smoking and betel chewing deposits.

Gokhale was keen that I settle down in Bombay, practice at the bar, and assist him in public work. After receiving a remittance from Natal, which I was awaiting, I set forth for Bombay. I hired chambers in the Fort and a house in Girgaum but God wouldn't let me settle in Bombay. My second son Manilal, just ten years old, was afflicted by typhoid combined

with pneumonia. After my son had recovered, I returned to Bombay, continuing my practice and getting familiar with Gokhale's style of work. But just when I was settling down in Bombay, I received a cable from South Africa: "Chamberlain expected here. Please return immediately".

I requested for funds that were provided immediately. I gave up my practice and journeyed for South Africa, leaving my wife and children in Bombay. The separation was painful but had to be done. On reaching Durban, I learnt that the date to wait on Mr. Chamberlain had been fixed. I had to draft the memorial to be submitted to him and accompany the deputation.

Chapter Seventeen

South African Diaries

Mr. Chamberlain had come to obtain a gift of 35 million pounds from South Africa and to win English hearts. Hence, he gave us a cold shoulder. We were disappointed as he advised us to please the Europeans if we wished to live in their midst. I followed Mr. Chamberlain to the Transvaal but was denied the opportunity to meet him there. Johannesburg was the stronghold of the Asiatic officers. But this Asiatic department was anti-Asian instead of protecting their own kind from the Europeans. I decided not to leave the Transvaal before removing this evil. I began collecting evidence and approached the Police Commissioner after that. He was convinced with my evidence. But he put forth the argument about the futility of convincing a white jury to convict a white offender against the evidence provided by coloured men. "But criminals cannot get away scot-free," he stated. "We must try!"

But although the police commissioner arrested the men, they were declared not guilty and acquitted. I was disappointed but took comfort from the fact that the government cashiered both officers as their crimes were too strong to ignore. So, the Asiatic department became relatively clean. I had nothing personal against these officers and helped them when they approached me in dire straits. They had an employment offer at the Johannesburg Municipality, only if I did not oppose their recruitment. I agreed, and this made every official act in a friendly manner towards me. I learnt later that this action was an essential part of both Satyagraha and Ahimsa. While it is right to attack a system, it is not right to attack its author as it is the same as attacking oneself. To harm another person is equal to harming the whole world as we are all children of the same Creator.

I'm not writing this autobiography to please critics. It is one of the experiments with truth. The truth is that just as the Indians in Durban were like family members to me, so were the English friends there. Meanwhile, it was getting increasingly difficult to cope up with both professional and public work. I had to employ a stenographer, and hired a Scottish girl called Miss Dick through an agent. Before long, she had become more of a daughter and a friend than a stenotypist. Not only was she efficient in managing funds worth thousands of pounds but was also in charge of account books. She won my total confidence and confided to me her innermost thoughts and feelings. I was fortunate to give her away in marriage and sadly, she left me after becoming Mrs. Macdonald. But

even after marriage, she always rushed to help me whenever I was under pressure. Her replacement was Miss Schlesin, about seventeen years old. She was a great replacement but was armed with a sharp tongue, speaking exactly what she felt. She refused to take a salary more than 10 pounds a month and used to scold me when I offered her more. "I'm not here to draw a salary," she would retort. "I'm here because I like working with you as well as your ideals."

She toiled night and day, and thousands of Indians sought her advice. She also led the Satyagraha movement single-handed when all the leaders were in jail. No wonder Gokhale gave Miss Schlesin the first place among all my Indian and European co-workers.

A gold mine near Johannesburg was responsible for the outbreak of the Black Plague. Most of the workers here were Negroes. A few were also Indians, and one day, twenty-three of them caught the infection and returned to their quarters. A brave man named Sjt. Madanjit sent a note to me for help, breaking open the lock of a vacant house, and keeping all the patients there. I rushed to the scene, and so did Dr. William Godfrey, who was both doctor and nurse to the patients. But the three of us were too less to handle so many patients. I took the help of four of my associates, and we toiled all night to save the patients. The Town Clerk thanked me for having saved the patients. The Municipality gave me a vacant godown to keep the patients. This godown was so dirty that we cleaned it ourselves. With the help of charitable Indians, we raised money for beds and other essentials to create a temporary hospital. The Municipality also lent us a nurse, and Dr. Godfrey was in charge. We had received instructions to give the patients frequent doses of brandy, but unfortunately none of them would touch brandy. I decided to put the three willing patients under the earth treatment, and two of them were saved. The remaining twenty died in the godown. The nurse caught the disease and died as well, and it's a mystery how we survived.

The Zulu Rebellion broke out in Natal while I was in Johannesburg. I did not bear any grudge against the Zulus as they hadn't harmed any Indians. But I doubted the cause of the rebellion as I believed then that the British Empire wanted to do good for the world. I wrote to the Governor of Natal, offering the services of an Indian Ambulance Corps, which was accepted immediately. I collected a contingent of twenty-four people and was given the temporary rank of Sergeant Major.

The reason for the rebellion was the refusal of a Zulu chief to pay a new tax imposed on his people. My heart was with the Zulus, and I was delighted to learn that we were to nurse the wounded Zulus as white people were unwilling to nurse them. The Zulus were very happy, but the white soldiers used to peep through the railings separating us and ask us not to treat the wounded Zulus. When we paid them

no attention, they rained abuses on the Zulus. Soon, I became friends with these soldiers, and the abuses stopped. We were soon discharged after the trouble blew over, and the Governor wrote to me thanking us for our services.

I started the Tolstoy Farm in Johannesburg with the help of a few friends like Mr. Kallenbach, where young Indian boys and girls were educated. There were no servants on the farm and everyone had to do all the work themselves. We laid stress on literary training, vocational training, physical training, spiritual training and character building.

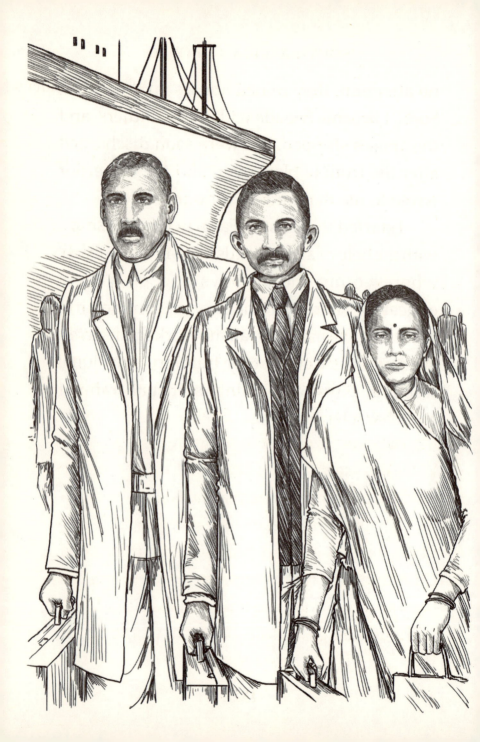

Chapter Eighteen

The War

In 1914, after the end of the Satyagraha struggle, I received Gokhale's instructions to return home via London. Kasturba, Kallenbach and I set sail for London. Upon entering the English Channel, we received word about the outbreak of the War. We reached London on 6th August, two days after war had been declared.

I learned that Gokhale was stranded in Paris, where he had gone for health issues. Communication between London and Paris had been severed, and I did not want to return home without seeing Gokhale. But what would I do in England till Gokhale returned? I believed that

THE WAR

Indians living in England should volunteer for the war just like the English students had. This met with opposition from the resident Indians as we were slaves and they were masters according to some. It was the duty of the slave to make himself free at the master's ill time. I did not share this opinion then as I did not believe that we had been reduced to slavery. I felt we could improve our status with the help of the British and should stand by them in their hour of need.

I assembled eighty volunteers, and wrote to Lord Crewe, offering our services for ambulance work. He accepted after slight hesitation and thanked us. We were examined in six weeks and put under military drill and training. The old, the infirm and the women were given the task of cutting and making clothes and dressings for the wounded. A ladies' club called the Lyceum volunteered to make as many clothes for the soldiers as they could. Shrimati Sarojini Naidu was a member of this club, and she threw herself

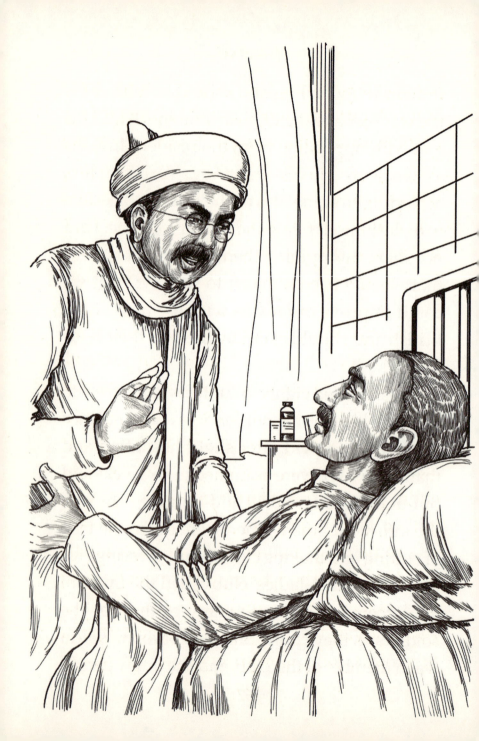

heart and soul into this project. People from South Africa questioned the justification of my participation in the war as it went against my principle of Ahimsa. My reasoning was when a war broke out, the duty of a follower of Ahimsa is to stop the war. I had also hoped to enhance the reputation of my people with the British Empire by my actions. Even today, I see no flaw in my actions.

Gokhale returned to London soon. I had suffered from an attack of pleurisy in England. I refused to go on a diet of milk and cereals as advised by my doctor. I even went against Gokhale's advice to go on a diet of milk products and meat as it went against my principles. The entire process of milking cows and buffaloes to their last drop of milk to feed human needs was something I was averse to. Gokhale finally decided to head back home, unable to withstand the October fogs of London. As it got chillier, I was advised by my doctors to go home as the cold would worsen my condition. So, I

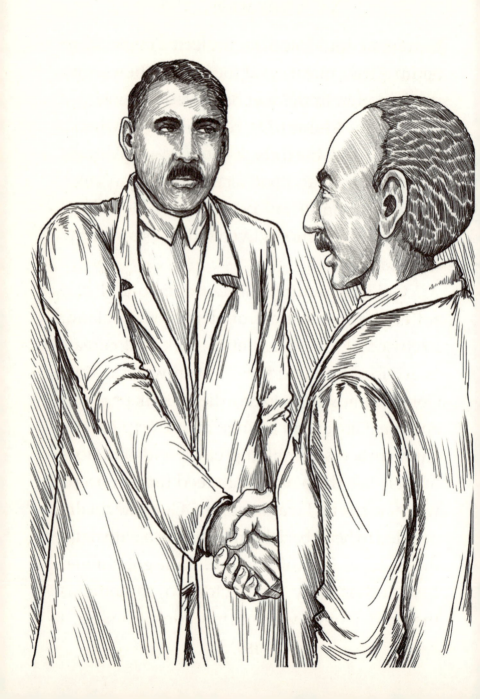

THE WAR

decided to return to India. Mr. Kallenbach had accompanied me to England as he wanted to visit India with me. But as he was of German origin, he was not issued a passport because Germans were under strict surveillance. It was a great pain to part from my good friend, Mr. Kallenbach. But it was clear that his pain was greater as he would have loved to lead the simple life of a farmer and weaver in India. Instead, he had to return to South Africa and work as an architect.

Chapter Nineteen

Back to India

It was such a joy when we landed in Bombay as it was almost an exile of ten years before returning to the motherland. After a brief stay in Bombay, I was summoned to Poona by Gokhale. He and the other members of the Servants of India Society showered me with affection. Gokhale was very eager, as I was, that I should join the Society. But the other members were hesitant as there was a vast difference between my ideals and work methods and theirs, although they had great love and respect for me.

    A group of my friends and followers had followed me from South Africa, and I requested

Gokhale to provide me an ashram where I could reside with them. I would prefer the ashram being somewhere in Gujarat. Gokhale liked the idea that I should serve the country from Gujarat, being a Gujarati. I was delighted when Gokhale offered to raise the expenses of the ashram himself.

From Poona, I travelled to Rajkot and Porbandar to meet my relatives. Then, I went to Shantiniketan where the Phoenix family from South Africa (my friends from the Phoenix Ashram) had been assigned separate quarters. I quickly mixed with the students and teachers of Shantiniketan, urging them to engage in self-help. I advised them to do away with paid cooks and servants and do the work themselves. The opinions were mixed, and when I asked the poet for his opinion, he said he was open to it if the teachers agreed. The boys were all eager for this experiment, and to them the poet said, "This experiment contains the key to Swaraj."

This was not easy and continued with success for some time before being eventually dropped. But there was nothing to lose from this experiment. I would have loved to stay on in Shantiniketan but received a telegram from Poona only after a week's stay there. It announced Gokhale's death. The whole of Shantiniketan mourned this national loss, and the same day I left for Poona accompanied by my wife and my associate, Maganlal Gandhi.

We reached Poona, and after the '*shraddha*' ceremonies were concluded, we began discussion on my joining the Society. I felt it was my duty to join to please Gokhale's spirit. The Society was divided into two sections; one in favour of my joining and one against it. The latter had no bitterness towards me, and only opposed because my principles would imperil the very objectives on which the Society had been formed. After long discussions, we dispersed, with the decision postponed to a later date.

Later, I decided to withdraw my application so that those opposed to me would be saved from making an awkward decision. They appreciated this gesture and our friendship became greater. My withdrawal made me a member of the Society, although not a formal one. Although I was not an official member, I was a member in spirit. Spiritual relationship is more precious than a physical one. When physical relationship is divorced from a spiritual one, it is like a body without a soul.

Chapter Twenty

Religious Excursions

I travelled to Rangoon to meet Dr. Mehta, halting at Calcutta first where I was a guest of the late Babu Bhupendranath Basu. Bengali hospitality reached its zenith here. I was a strict fruitarian those days, and the best fruit and nuts available in Calcutta were ordered for me. The ladies of the house were awake all-night skinning various fruits for me, and this kind of attention was very embarrassing, but inescapable.

After Rangoon, I left for Haridwar. The year was 1915, and the year of the *Kumbha Mela* (Fair) held once every twelve years. I was not keen on the fair, but on meeting Mahatma Munshiramji, in his Gurukul. I joined Gokhale's Society's Volunteer Corps deployed for service at the Kumbh.

At the Kumbh, I was exposed to the hypocrisy more than the devotion. The swarm of sadhus who had descended there, seemed keen to enjoy the good things in life above all else. I was stunned when I saw a cow with five feet! I learned that the poor cow was a sacrifice to the wickedness of man. A foot had been cut off from a live calf and grafted on the shoulder of the cow to fleece innocent pilgrims of their money.

Meeting Mahatma Munshiramji was a lovely experience, and his ashram was quiet compared to the din of the Kumbh. He received me with great affection, and here I was introduced to Acharya Ramadevji, a powerful personality. We had long discussions about various subjects, like introducing industrial training in the Gurukul. Although we differed in opinion on many matters, we forged a strong friendship.

I had heard much about the Lakshman Jhula, a hanging bridge over the Ganges, a little distance from Hrishikesh. I decided to visit and was overwhelmed by the sheer beauty of Nature. But I was disturbed at the way people were dirtying these beauty spots.

I had to set up my ashram in India, and these small journeys helped me decide in a small way where I would live and what I would do. The Satyagraha Ashram was founded on 25 May 1915 in Ahmedabad, the chosen one from many other cities. There were many reasons for this. Gujarat was always on my preferred list, and the capital of Gujarat was also the centre of wealth. Monetary help from wealthy citizens would always be available. It was also an ancient centre for handloom weaving, and perfect for the revival of the cottage industry of hand-spinning.

At the time, there were twenty-five men and women with me from South Africa and various parts of India. We started the Ashram

together. The trouble erupted when we agreed to accept a family of three into our ashram. This was a family of untouchables, and this created a division between us and the people who had been financially aiding the ashram. All monetary help was stopped, and rumours of social boycott followed. We held on, but soon all our funds dried up.

Then, a miracle happened. During many such tough times, God has sent help at the last moment. One of the children informed me that a Seth was waiting in a car outside and wanted to see me. I went outside to meet him.
"I want to provide some help to the ashram," the Sheth declared. "Will you take it?"
"Certainly," I replied, confessing, "I'm almost at the end of my resources now."
The man left, declaring that he would come the next day at the same time. He arrived at the appointed time and waited for me outside in the car. After I went out, he placed notes worth Rs. 13,000 in my hand and drove away.

This help was totally unexpected, and that too from a perfect stranger. No enquiries at all. Just rendering help and leaving. We were safe for a year now. The admission of the family of untouchables was a valuable lesson to the ashram. Initially, the other women, including my wife, did not like the idea of untouchables eating and living with us. The fact that orthodox Hindus came forward to help the ashram proved that the very foundations of untouchability had been shaken.

Chapter Twenty-One

Champaran

Champaran, the land of King Janaka, was full of indigo plantations till 1931. The Champaran tenant was bound by law to plant three out of every twenty parts of his land with indigo for his landlord. This was known as the tinkanthia system, as three kanthas out of twenty (one acre) had to have indigo planted.

Rajkumar Shukla was one of the agriculturalists who faced this hardship, and he was keen to remove this indigo stain for thousands of sufferers like himself. He met me in Lucknow, where I visited for the Congress of 1916, and requested me to help him. He invited

me to Champaran to see the problem with my own eyes. I went to Cawnpore from Lucknow, and the man persistently followed me there, pleading for the cause. I promised to come later. But when I returned to the Ashram, he was there as well, requesting me to fix a time for my visit. I told him to come to Calcutta when I visited and take me from there.

When I reached Bhupen Babu's place in Calcutta, I found that Rajkumar Shukla had already established himself there. I gave in to the resolute farmer and accompanied him to Champaran. We reached Patna in the morning, and it was my first visit there. Using my London contacts, I met some eminent Biharis who agreed to help in my cause. In Champaran, I sought meetings with the planters as well as the Commissioner of the Division to get both sides of the story, which was granted. The Secretary of the Planter's Association branded me as an outsider who had no business to interfere between the farmers and their tenants. I politely

CHAMPARAN

informed him that I wasn't an outsider, but a representative of the tenants.

I called on the Commissioner, who bullied me and advised me to leave immediately. I started for Motihari, the headquarters of Champaran, with my co-workers but was served a notice to leave Champaran immediately. I wrote back saying that I wouldn't leave Champaran till my enquiry was finished. A summons was issued to me to receive my trial for disobeying the notice. The news of the notice and the summons spread like wildfire, and Motihari's men came out in my support. The crowd followed me wherever I went, and the relationship between me and the officials also improved. They saw that I was not offending them personally but was offering civil resistance to their notices. They also extended help in regulating the crowds. Earlier, no one knew me in Champaran, which was cut off from the rest of India, being right at the foot of the Himalayas, and close to Nepal.

CHAMPARAN

But the Magistrate postponed the judgement. The Lieutenant Governor ordered the case against me to be withdrawn and the Collector wrote to me asking me to proceed with my enquiry, and take any official help needed. Thus, the country had its first taste of Civil Disobedience. I knew the planters and officials were displeased at the Government stance.

That day in Champaran was a historic, unforgettable, red-letter day for me and the peasants. Ironically, I was supposed to be on trial, but it was the Government which found itself on trial instead. The Commissioner had ensnared the Government in the very net he had spread out for me.

Chapter Twenty-Two

Penetrating the Villages

I realised that proper village education was the first step towards long-term work in Bihar. I decided to open primary schools in six villages. The villagers would provide boarding and lodging for the teachers while we would see to the other expenses.

Hiring local teachers wouldn't help. So, I issued a public appeal for voluntary teachers, and received a steady response. Soon, a strong contingent was assembled, and teaching cleanliness and good manners was laid stress upon. We also focussed on sanitary work to remove dirt and filth.

PENETRATING THE VILLAGES

Each school was entrusted to the charge of one man and one woman in terms of medical relief and sanitation. Medical relief was a simple affair with a doctor visiting each centre in turn. But sanitation was challenging as people did not want to do anything on their own. But our volunteers swept the roads and surroundings, cleaned the wells, filled up pools and enlisted villagers as volunteers slowly. Meanwhile, the time to leave Bihar had come as the purpose of this visit had been achieved. The tinkathia system, in place for almost a century, was finally abolished in Champaran, bringing an end to planter's rule. It was my earnest desire to penetrate more villages in Bihar as the early ground had been prepared. But God willed otherwise, and I had to leave Bihar.

I had received an intimation from Ahmedabad, regarding the agitation of the labourers there. Wages were low and I was requested to guide them. I had also received a request to guide the peasants in Kheda district

where there was a crop failure. I wanted to deal with these two matters quickly and return to Champaran to finish the work I had started there. But sadly, things moved slowly in Ahmedabad, and I was unable to return to Champaran on time, with the result that the schools closed one by one.

In Ahmedabad, I advised the mill labourers to go on strike after speaking with them at length and understanding their problems. However, I put certain conditions like never engaging in violence, not to depend on alms, and to remain firm even it meant earning bread and butter through other honest means. My suggestions were accepted, and it was during this strike that I became intimate with leaders like Vallabhbhai Patel and Shankarlal Banker.

The strike went on for twenty-one days. I met the mill-owners during this time and pleaded the cause of the labourers. I could sense that the labourers were close to breaking point, and about to break their vow of non-violence. I

had to do something!

"I will not touch any food till a settlement of the strike is reached," I declared. The labourers were shocked and offered to fast themselves.

"There is no need for you to fast," I replied. "To remain true to your pledge of non-violence is enough for the cause."

I began my fast as the last alternative to end the strike. On the first day, many labourers joined me in fasting. But I convinced them not to fast from the second day and fasted alone. An atmosphere of goodwill was created all around, and this also touched the hearts of the mill-owners. The strike ended after I had fasted for only three days as a settlement was reached. Sweets were distributed by the mill-owners to the labours to celebrate.

An amusing incident occurred during the distribution of sweets which had arrived in large quantities to be distributed among the labourers. The beggar population of Ahmedabad arrived in large numbers on hearing of the ceremony,

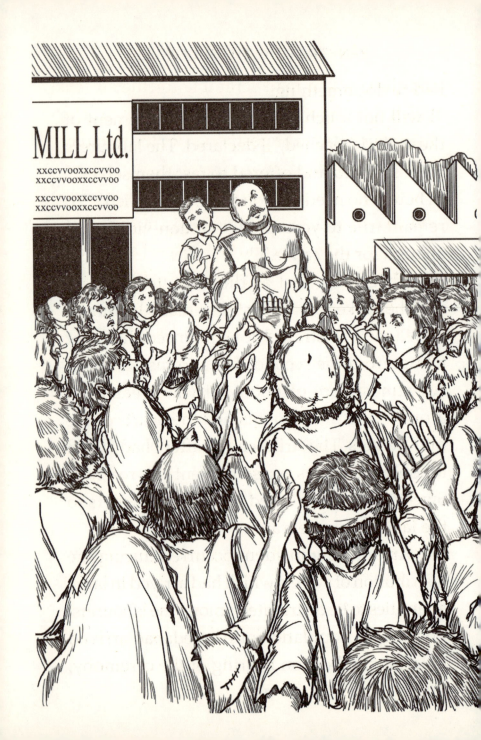

and there was a mad scramble for the sweets which were being distributed in the open. The distribution had to be postponed for the next day from the controlled environment of a bungalow. The poverty and starvation of India drives more and more people to become beggars each day. They lose all decency and self-respect after that. It is the fault of our philanthropists who provide them with alms instead of providing work for them, and for not insisting that they work for their bread instead of begging.

Chapter Twenty-Three

The Kheda Satyagraha

I dived into the Kheda Satyagraha as soon as the Ahmedabad mill strike ended. Widespread failure of crops in the Kheda district had resulted in famine, and the Patidars of Kheda wanted the revenue assessment of the year suspended. Under the Land Revenue Rules, the cultivators could claim full suspension of the revenue assessment for the year if the crop was four annas or under. The Government claimed that the cultivation was above four annas, while the cultivators claimed that it was under four annas.

THE KHEDA SATYAGRAHA

Vallabhbhai Patel, who was part of this agitation, sacrificed a thriving career at the bar for the cause. The rich Gujaratis were ready to offer monetary help for the Kheda cause. They did not realise that Satyagraha could not be obtained solely on the strength of riches. In fact, money is the least needed in this struggle. We went from village to village explaining the basic principles of Satyagraha.

The main thing to educate the agriculturists was that the officials were not their masters, but servants of the people and the country. The Government began coercion when the struggle refused to subside. The officers sold people's cattle and grabbed whatever they could lay their hands on. This made the peasants nervous, and some paid up their dues while others continued the fight.

The Kheda Satyagraha ended unexpectedly. A big Mamlatdar sent word that the poorer

Patidars would be exempted if the well-to-do ones paid up the money. This was agreed upon, but I was not satisfied at this end as it was not a graceful one. But the fact was that the Kheda Satyagraha marked the beginning of the peasant awakening in Gujarat in terms of their political education.

Chapter Twenty-Four

Rescued from Death

The Viceroy, Lord Chelmsford invited several leaders for a war conference in Delhi because of the crisis that threatened the British Empire. I attended the same, although I had reservations about the conference because of the exclusion of the Ali Brothers, who were in jail. I had met them a couple of times but had heard much about their courage and service. I understood the need for Hindu Muslim unity in India and was always ready to befriend patriotic Muslims to understand the Muslim mind better. My application to meet the Ali Brothers in jail had sadly not borne fruit. When I was invited by

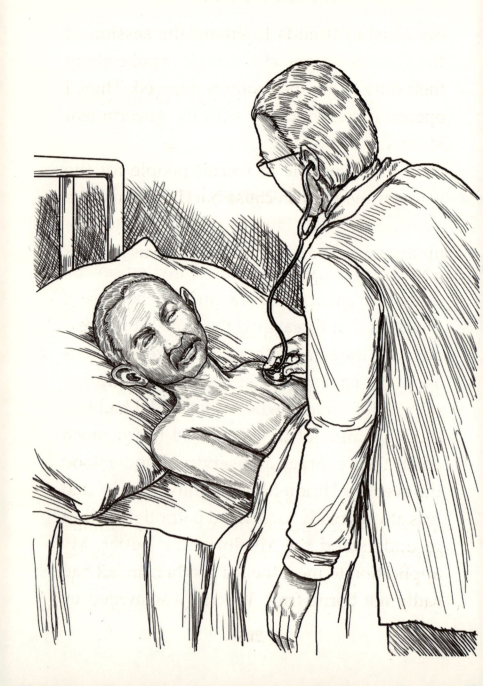

RESCUED FROM DEATH

my Muslim friends to attend the session of the Muslim League at Calcutta, I spoke about their duty to get the brothers released. Then, I opened correspondence with the government for their release.

I asked people to recruit people for the war and the English cause but did not receive a good response. "How can you ask us to take up arms being an advocate of Ahimsa?" was the persistent question.

My health suffered during the recruiting campaign. I suffered an acute attack of dysentery, and while I tossed and turned in pain on my bed at the Ashram, Vallabhbhai brought the news of Germany's defeat in the war. I was sure that I was near death as my illness grew worse. I lay waiting for death when I was revived by a strange person. Dr. Talvalkar brought him from Maharashtra and he was not a famous doctor. He had almost finished his course of studies in Grant Medical College without taking his degree. Later, I learned that he was

a member of the Brahmo Samaj and his name was Sjt. Kelkar. He swore by the ice treatment, which he wanted to try on me. I gave him the name of "The Ice Doctor' and permitted him to experiment on my body. Kelkar's treatment involved the application of ice all over the body. I don't know if this treatment was effective as he claimed, but it strengthened my mind, which worked on the body to make it strong as well. My appetite returned and I could walk as well.

Chapter Twenty-Five

The Rowlatt Bills

I had grown extremely weak because of my dysentery. Shankarlal Banker urged me to consult Dr. Dalal, who advised a milk diet to become stronger. When I told him the reason for my aversion towards milk and how cows and buffaloes were stripped of their last ounce of milk, he suggested goat's milk. I gave in as I wanted to live to finish the Satyagraha movement.

My health improved after Dr. Dalal performed an operation on me. I was just recovering when I read about the Rowlatt Committee's report in the newspaper, which surprised me greatly. I went to Ahmedabad where I voiced my concern to Vallabhbhai. We held a meeting to counter the Rowlatt Committee report and the Satyagraha Sabha was formed with me as President. As our agitation against the report grew, the Government appeared keener to implement its recommendations, and the Rowlatt Bill was published. During the debate on this bill in the Indian Legislative Assembly, Lal Bahadur Shastri delivered a passionate speech with a warning to the Government. Even the Viceroy heard it spellbound.

The Bill had not been made into an Act, and I travelled to Madras on an invitation from Rajagopalachari to counter the Bill. While I discussed the matter with leaders in Madras, the Rowlatt Bill was published as an Act. I went to sleep disappointed, and the idea appeared to me in between a state of sleep and consciousness, as if in a dream. In the morning, I told Rajagopalachari my idea, "We should call upon the country to observe a general *hartal*. Let

THE ROWLATT BILLS

the Indian people suspend their entire business for a day as a sign of protest to fast and pray." Rajagopalachari loved my idea, and so did my other friends. The day of the hartal was fixed on 6 April 1919. The entire nation, including towns and villages a complete hartal that day. It was an amazing spectacle. I returned to Bombay and decided to begin Civil Disobedience by publishing two of my books and selling them openly. We explained to the people that this literature was forbidden to be bought or sold by the Government and could invite imprisonment. But the people now had no fear of being jailed and the copies sold like hot cakes. I was on my way to Delhi and Amritsar when I heard of my probable arrest at Mathura. I was prohibited by the police to enter Punjab and arrested at Palwal railway station. I was escorted back to Bombay as a 'gentleman prisoner'. Later, I learned that my arrest had angered the people to a mad frenzy. My colleagues asked me to reach Pydhuni at once, where huge crowds

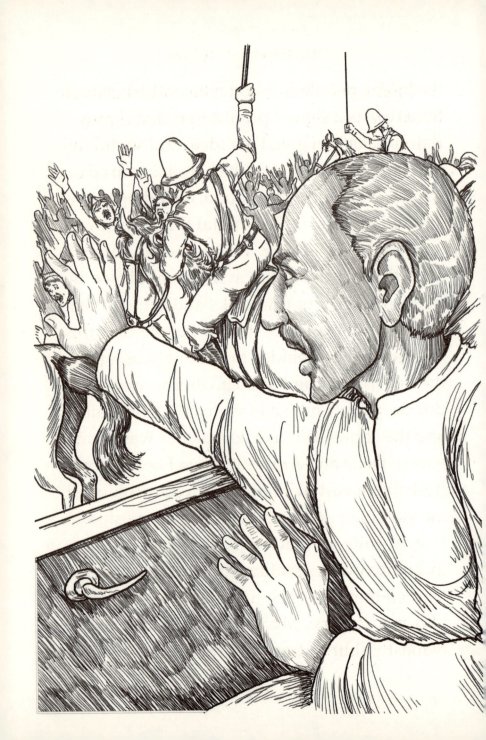

THE ROWLATT BILLS

had gathered. Only I could pacify them. People went mad with joy on seeing me, and chants of Vande Mataram and Allaho Akbar pierced the skies. The crowd started raining brickbats from above the buildings as they saw a convoy of mounted police. I urged them to be calm, but it was too late! The mounted police charged at the crowd, and a stampede ensued as people tried to flee. Our motor managed to pass as people were trampled underfoot and mauled. It was a dreadful scene with people and horsemen joined in a melee. I immediately complained to the Commissioner about the conduct of the police. We argued with each other as he thought he had been right in issuing the orders. I decided to suspend Satyagraha as violence had no part in it, especially from the people.

I also realised my mistake. For normal people to understand the deeper implications of Satyagraha, they had to be trained first. I raised a corps of Satyagrahi volunteers and started educating the common people about the inner

THE ROWLATT BILLS

meaning and significance of Satyagraha. But as the number of fresh recruits began to dwindle each day instead of growing, I realised I had a tough task at hand to train people in civil disobedience.

Chapter Twenty-Six

Congress Initiation

Things erupted in Punjab with the Jallianwala Bagh tragedy, and I was not permitted to enter Punjab. Ironically, Sir Michael O' Dwyer held me responsible for the trouble in Punjab. Some angry young Punjabis also held me responsible for the martial law. They felt that if I hadn't suspended civil disobedience, the Jallianwala Bagh massacre wouldn't have taken place. They threatened me with assassination if I entered Punjab.

But I was keen on visiting Punjab as I had never been there. But each time, I was stopped by the Viceroy when I asked for permission. I was finally allowed to visit and when I arrived at Lahore, a sea of humanity awaited me at the railway station. They were mad with joy as if meeting a relative after ages. The Punjab Government was forced to release the hundreds of prisoners jailed because of martial law. The Ali Brothers arrived from jail when Congress opened. Pandit Motilal Nehru was President of the Punjab Congress. I also had the opportunity to interact with Pandit Malaviyaji.

The King's announcement on the new reforms had just been issued, and even though they were not fully satisfactory to me, I felt we should accept them as the signs were positive with the Ali Brothers being released. But they were not satisfactory to everyone else, including veterans like the late Lokmanya and Deshbandhu Chittaranjan Das. I could not bear to differ from such revered leaders and offered to absent myself from the Congress. But the senior leaders did not agree. When the day arrived, I framed my resolution and moved it with a trembling heart. Malaviyaji and Mr. Jinnah supported it. Jeramdas then handed over his amendment to me and pleaded with the delegates to avoid a division. I was in favour of Jeramdas's amendment.

"If C.R. Das approves, I have no objection," Lokmanya declared. Deshbandhu was thawed at last and glanced at Sjt. Bepin Chandra Pal for an endorsement. Malaviyaji snatched away the amendment, and before a definite 'yes' was procured from Deshbandhu, he shouted, "Brother delegates, you will be happy to know that a compromise has been reached."

This compromise further increased my responsibility in the Congress. In fact, my participation in the Amritsar Congress was my real initiation into the Congress. Two things that I wanted to do in the first year was raising funds for the Jallianwala Bagh memorial and to work as a draftsman for the Congress. I knew I had an aptitude for these two tasks. I also took the responsibility of framing the constitution on one

condition. The two most popular leaders with the public, Lokmanya Tilak and Deshbandhu Chittaranjan Das should be associated with me on the committee for framing the constitution. But as they were busy leaders, each should appoint a trusted representative to be with me on the committee. This suggestion was accepted and Sjt. Kelkar and I.B. Sen were appointed as proxies. We presented a unanimous report, and I am proud of this constitution. If we could fully work out this constitution, I'm confident it would bring us Swaraj. As I assumed this responsibility, I made my real entrance into Congress politics.

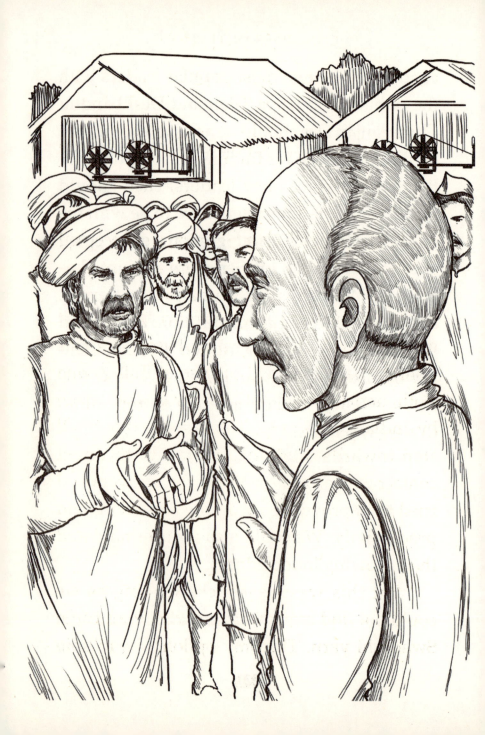

Chapter Twenty-Seven

Khadi and the Spinning Wheel

We had envisioned long ago to wear cloth that was created by our own hands. Everyone in the Ashram had discarded the use of mill-woven cloth, and we resolved to wear clothes made by Indian yarn only. This was also a small step towards attaining Swaraj. With direct contact we gauged the life of the weavers and tried to improve their working conditions and productivity. We could also reduce fraud and their growing indebtedness.

But this was clearly challenging as we could not find many weavers who would spin Swadeshi yarn. The only option was to spin

our own yarn and earn independence from the mill owners. In 1917, I met the remarkable lady called Gangabehn Majumdar, who promised to find me the ancient spinning wheel I was desperately looking for. She was a woman of means who had limited needs, and served the suppressed class, often riding alone on horseback. She found the spinning wheel in Vijapur in the Baroda state after an extensive search through Gujarat. Many people had spinning wheels in their houses here but had kept them in their lofts as useless articles. They were willing to use them again if someone promised to buy their yarn and supply them with slivers regularly.

We procured the sliver from a mill-owner but so much yarn began to be delivered that we were at a loss what to do with it. But we could not depend on the generosity of the mill-owner. Gangabehn came to the rescue once again to find carders who could supply slivers. She engaged a carder to card cotton and trained a

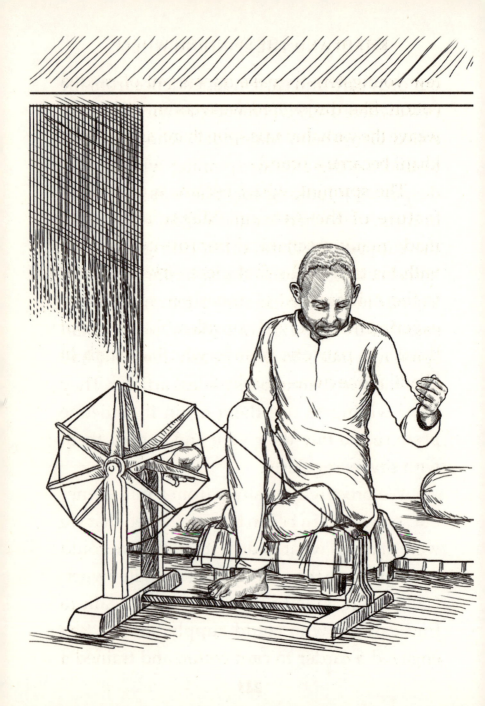

few youngsters to make slivers out of carded cotton. She discovered weavers in Vijapur to weave the yarn that was spun there, and Vijapur khadi became a brand.

The spinning wheel became a prominent feature of the Ashram. Maganlal Gandhi made many mechanical improvements on it with his talent. The first piece of khadi made in the Ashram cost 17 annas per yard. These experiments involved considerable costs, but thanks to patriotic friends who had faith in khadi, money was supplied.

Chapter Twenty-Eight

The Non-Cooperation Resolution

The All-India Congress Committee prepared to hold a special session of the Congress in 1920 to deliberate on the non-cooperation resolution. Lala Lajpat Rai was elected President. I was nervous as I did not know who would support the resolution and who would oppose it. It was suggested by the veterans that the demand for Swaraj be added in my resolution, which was passed after a tiring, stormy and serious discussion.

The resolutions adopted at the special session of the Calcutta Congress were to be confirmed at its annual session at Nagpur. After

THE NON-COOPERATION RESOLUTION

a few amendments, the resolution was passed unanimously. The resolution regarding the revision of the Congress constitution was part of the agenda. The question of the Congress goal was discussed keenly. In the constitution presented by me, the Congress goal was attaining Swaraj within the British Empire if possible, and without, if needed. A section of the Congress wanted to limit attaining Swaraj within the British Empire only. This was put forth by Malaviyaji and Mr. Jinnah but they could not get many votes. The proposal that Swaraj was to be got by peaceful and legitimate means was opposed with the argument that the means to be adopted shouldn't have any restrictions. But Congress chose to adopt the original draft after a frank and lengthy discussion. Resolutions about Hindu-Muslim unity, eradication of untouchability, and khadi were also passed in this Congress.

Chapter Twenty-Nine

Farewell

It is time now to bring these chapters to a close. From this point onwards, my life has been so public that there is nothing people are unaware of. All I can say is that I have tried to give a faithful narrative. This exercise has given me absolute mental peace. I can only hope it brings faith in Truth and Ahimsa to waverers. To see God or Truth face to face, one must love the meanest of creatures as oneself. Self-purification is important as God cannot be realised by someone who's not pure of heart. Self-purification implies purification in all walks of life, and purification of oneself leads

FAREWELL

to purification of one's surroundings. But the road of self-purification is steep and difficult. One must be totally passion-free in thought, speech and action and rise above emotions like love and hatred, attachment and repulsion. The knowledge that dormant passions still exist within me have humiliated me, but I haven't given up on my goal. I'm aware that I have a difficult path ahead of me. I must reduce myself to zero. If a man does not put himself willingly at the end of the line of his fellow creatures, there is no hope of salvation for him. Ahimsa is the ultimate limit of humility. I shall bid farewell to the reader now, for the time being, asking him to join me in prayer to the God of Truth- May he grant me the boon of Ahimsa in mind, word and deed.

THE STORY OF MY EXPERIMENTS WITH TRUTH

About the Author

▪ Mohandas Karamchand Gandhi

Mohandas Karamchand Gandhi was born on 2 October 1869 in Porbandar, India. Through nonviolent resistance, Gandhi helped India win her freedom from British rule. He was one of the most respected leaders of the 1900s, earning the title of Mahatma (Great Soul) and Father of the Nation. Some of the personalities that influenced Gandhi greatly were Jesus Christ, Thoreau, Tolstoy and Ruskin Bond.

Gandhi was the victim of child marriage, marrying Kasturba when both were thirteen years old. The couple had four children. Gandhi was sent to study law in London and returned to India in 1891 to practice. But when his law career failed to take off, he undertook a one-year contract to do legal work in South Africa.

Gandhi stayed for 21 years in South Africa, working tirelessly for the rights of the Indians settled there. The seeds of the famous method of action called Satyagraha based upon the principles of non-violence, truth, civil disobedience and courage were sown here. Gandhi deemed Satyagraha as the vehicle to obtain social and political goals.

Gandhi returned to India in 1915, and within 15 years he rose to become the leader of the Indian Nationalist Movement.

The Story of My Experiments with Truth is Gandhi's autobiography, covering the journey from his birth in 1869 to the year 1921. No wonder that it is the world's largest selling autobiography.

THE STORY OF MY EXPERIMENTS WITH TRUTH

■ Questions

Chapter 1
- Describe the incident with young Gandhi when Mr. Giles, the Educational Inspector came to visit his school?
- Which story book left an everlasting impression on young Gandhi's mind and how? Explain in detail.

Chapter 2
- Why was Gandhi ashamed of having married? Explain his views.
- What were the two different rites in Kathiawad? What was the difference between the two?

Chapter 3
- What was Gandhi's view on handwriting? Explain
- Describe the incident between Gandhi and the Sanskrit teacher. What were Gandhi's views on Sanskrit?

Chapter 4
- How did Gandhi become a meat-eater? Describe the incident.
- How did Gandhi abstain from meat eating?

Chapter 5
- Why did Gandhi write a letter to his father? What was his father's reaction?
- Why was Gandhi sad, ashamed and miserable? What message does he give to all married men at the end of the chapter?

Chapter 6
- What did Gandhi get from the old servant of the family? Explain in detail.
- Explain why a young Gandhi disliked Christianity?

Chapter 7
- Who was Mavji Dave? What suggestion did he have for Gandhi's family and why?

THE STORY OF MY EXPERIMENTS WITH TRUTH

- Why were Gandhi's caste-people angry? Describe Gandhi's conversation with the community headman.

Chapter 8
- How and why did Gandhi cut his expenses by half?
- In which year did Gandhi visit Paris for the first time? Describe his trip briefly.

Chapter 9
- What shock did Gandhi receive after landing in India? Describe his feelings.
- Describe Gandhi's debut in the Small Causes Court.

Chapter 10
- Who sent a job offer for Gandhi? Describe what was written in the letter.
- Why were there no berths on the boat selling for Natal? How did Gandhi manage to get a berth for himself?

Chapter 11
- Why did Gandhi decide to stay back in Natal? Explain.
- Who was Balasundaram and why did he come to Gandhi for help? How did Gandhi help this man?

Chapter 12
- Why did Gandhi offer his services to the State? How did he help in the cause?
- Who were the people who Gandhi met in Calcutta and why?

Chapter 13
- Why was the steamer carrying Gandhi put on quarantine? Explain briefly.
- Why did the crowd attack Gandhi? Who saved him and how?

Chapter 14
- What is Brahmacharya? Why was Gandhi so keen on it?
- Why did Gandhi cut his hair himself? What was the reaction of his colleagues?

THE STORY OF MY EXPERIMENTS WITH TRUTH

Chapter 15
- Whom did Gandhi support during the Boer war and why? Do you think he was right in doing so?
- Why did Gandhi and his wife have a disagreement regarding the gifts given to them? Explain in detail.

Chapter 16
- Why did Gandhi decide to stay on in Calcutta? Whom did he stay with?
- Describe the difference between third-class railway compartments in Europe, India and South Africa according to Gandhi.

Chapter 17
- Who was Gandhi's first stenographer? What were Gandhi's views on her?
- How did the Black Plague break out? How did Gandhi help the victims?

Chapter 18
- How did Gandhi and his volunteers contribute during the war? Explain.
- Why was Gandhi advised a diet of milk products and meat? Why didn't he agree?

Chapter 19
- What experiment did Gandhi conduct at Shantiniketan? Do you think it was a good move?
- Why did Gandhi leave for Poona suddenly? Describe briefly what took place in Poona.

Chapter 20
- Briefly describe Gandhi's experiences at the Kumbh Mela.
- What was the case of the cow with five feet? Explain in detail.

Chapter 21
- Explain what the Tinkanthia system was.
- Who was Rajkumar Shukla? What was his request to Gandhi?

THE STORY OF MY EXPERIMENTS WITH TRUTH

Chapter 22
- *What were Gandhi's plans for long-term work in Bihar?*
- *Describe the amusing incident during the sweet distribution at the end of this chapter.*

Chapter 23
- *What was the Kheda Satyagraha?*
- *How did the Kheda Satyagraha come to an end?*

Chapter 24
- *Who was the 'Ice Doctor'? Why was he named thus?*
- *How did the 'Ice Doctor' save Gandhi's life?*

Chapter 25
- *How did Gandhi start having goat's milk and why?*
- *Why did Gandhi suspend Satyagraha? Was he right in doing so?*

Chapter 26
- *Describe how the King's new reforms were approved by the Indian leaders.*
- *What was the condition laid down by Gandhi to frame the constitution? How was this implemented finally and why?*

Chapter 27
- *Who was Gangabehn Majumdar? How did she help Gandhi?*
- *Describe how the Vijapur khadi became a brand.*

Chapter 28
- *Why was Gandhi nervous? Explain.*
- *Describe briefly the events that took place at the annual Congress session at Nagpur.*

Chapter 29
- *How can one realise God or Truth according to Gandhi?*
- *What is the one thing about Gandhi's teachings that you want to incorporate in your own life and why?*